WHO'S YOUR BABY DADDY

COMPLETE SEASON 2

STASIA BLACK

PART 1

ONE

HOPE

"THIS IS RIDICULOUS," Milo said, glaring at Leander. Then he looked at me. "Are you really going to let him do this to you?"

I lifted my head up from the pillow and then dropped it again. "You'll be here if I need anything, right? And it'll make *him* leave?" I gestured with my head at Leander.

Leander made a sort of growling noise low in his throat... and continued tying me to the bed.

Yes, I was letting him tie me to the bed.

Look, I'd just had a batshit night. I'd tried to sneak away from them, then finally admitted I was pregnant...with one of the twin's baby—though only God knew which twin. I was exhausted. Still nauseated. And after all that, ready to sleep for a hundred years. Or at least twenty-four hours.

Meanwhile, Leander had the Dubai premiere of his movie tonight. And he was actually going as himself instead of sending Janus. Maybe because he needed time away from me as much as I wanted it from him.

Or maybe he was going out tonight so he could fuck some other woman; the nasty thought sliced through my mind before I could stop it. The silken tie Leander was tying on my wrist cinched tighter but I didn't look up at him.

"If this is the only way I can be assured you won't run," he bent over to growl low in my ear, "so be it."

I couldn't help my sharp intake of breath at his closeness and the intensity in his words. They sounded possessive. *They weren't*, I had to remind myself. He just didn't trust me.

He hesitated there for a moment, our heads close together, breaths mingling. And then he yanked away to stand up straight again.

"I'll be at the stylist," Leander snapped to an unhappy Milo who was standing beside the bed. Janus brooded near the wall with his arms crossed. Leander pointed at each of them in turn. "Don't you dare let her free, either of you. I expect to find her in this exact same position when I get home."

Milo rolled his eyes and Janus flipped Leander off.

Leander just glared back. "I mean it." Then he grabbed his jacket, wallet, and was out of the room.

It felt like we all took a collective breath. Or maybe that was just me. Because almost as soon as the door shut, Janus was in motion, flying across the room towards the bed.

His fingers immediately started undoing the knots his brother had just tied.

"Janus!" I cried. "He just said—"

"Fuck him. I'm not tying up a pregnant woman. Especially one I helped knock up." Janus cupped the back of my head gently. Lovingly. "Letting him think he had his way was just the fastest way to get that asshole out of here."

Milo leapt into action, untying my ankles.

"I won't run again," I said, fighting back tears. What the hell? I usually never cried, and here I was suddenly a fountain. I bit them back but still they flowed. Damned hormones. "I swear I never meant for any of this to happen." I needed them to believe me.

Janus pulled my hand into his after he released it from the tie and rubbed it between his. Like he was trying to get circulation back into it even though I'd barely been tied up three minutes. His forehead furrowed. "I'm so sorry for my jackass brother. We'll make this all better. I swear. I swear we'll make it up to you."

He pulled me into a hug. His body was so warm and I clung to him.

I hadn't realized how much I needed this.

"Hey, hey, it's okay, I'm not going anywhere."

I only squeezed tighter. I couldn't talk. My throat was too choked up. I just squeezed the life out of Janus's neck.

And then there was another warm body at my back and Milo's arms came around me too.

"Shhhh, shhhh, it's okay, baby," Janus said. "It's okay to cry. You don't have to be strong for us. Cry on Daddy's chest, baby. You're so fierce the rest of the time. Let us be your strength for a little while." He stroked his fingers through my hair. "Just lay it all down. Lay it all down for once."

Was this the same man who loved to spank me until my ass was sore?

I sobbed into his chest and Milo rubbed soothing circles on my back. We all laid down on the bed, me sandwiched between them. They lulled me to sleep with their sweet, sweet caresses.

"SLEEPING BEAUTY, it's time to wake up."

Soft kisses landed on my eyelids. I blinked up to Janus and Milo's faces looming above me. I looked around, confused at first about where I was.

A hotel room, clearly.

And then it all rushed back. I wanted to reach for the covers and yank them back up over me.

"How are you feeling?" Milo asked. He held up a small box towards me. "Do you need a cracker? I've heard eating something before you get out of bed can help with the pregnancy nausea."·

I shook my head. So much information coming at me while I was cloudy with sleep wasn't helping.

"Bathroom," I mumbled.

"Of course," Milo said, and then there was a man on each side of me, *hauling* more than helping me out of bed.

"Oh well, okay, *oof*," I stumbled, then planted my feet. "I can make it to the bathroom on my own, you know?" I shook their grips off my arms. Milo let go but Janus didn't.

"I don't want you to fall," was all Janus said, still with his arm in mine.

I rolled my eyes. "Well, you aren't coming in with me."

He arched an eyebrow but I firmly shook my head.

By the time I'd done my business and come back out, I was still yawning and stretching. "What time is it anyway? How'd the premiere go?"

Janus and Milo exchanged a look. My stomach sank. What did *that* look mean?

"Oh God, did you wake me up because of some PR disaster?"

"What?" Janus said, then rapidly shook his head. "No, no. The premiere is still in an hour. We woke you up because we're all going."

My mouth dropped open as I looked out the window, only now realizing it was almost dark out. Leander had left this morning.

I shook my head, a nervous laugh escaping. "We can't. He expects me to still be tied to the frickin' bed."

I pointed back to the bed. The covers were twisted from the three of us sleeping for the past however many hours. It seemed pretty clear no one had been tied up. Yeep. Leander wasn't happy when people didn't follow his directions.

"Well, maybe it's time my brother starts learning he doesn't always call the shots." Janus pushed some hair behind my ear, eyes intense on mine. "That might not even be his baby in you. And I'm for damn sure not going to stand by while he disrespects the mother of my child. You deserve to be at that premiere just as much as he does."

"Um, well, technically, he's the star of the movie and I'm just his publi—"

"Shower up, buttercup," Janus interrupted, a huge grin on his face. "We've got a premiere to crash. It's time to make a statement about who's really in charge here."

TWO

HOPE

"I CAN'T BELIEVE you two are making me do this," I hissed underneath my breath as our car dropped us off and security vetted our press passes.

"We can't make you do anything, Hope," Milo said, eyes darting around. "And we never want to." He was looking particularly dashing in a tux and silver tie. "You always have a choice."

I huffed out a laugh and smoothed out my dress for the thousandth time even though there weren't any wrinkles in it after I'd steamed it back at the hotel. "Easy for you to say. You weren't tied to a hotel bed earlier today."

"That's why we're here," Janus said. He hadn't left my side the entire time I'd gotten ready. Almost as if he was making up for Leander's leaving by sticking as close as a tick. It also meant he'd done sweet Dom things like comb my hair and shave and lotion my legs. He'd pampered me all to hell, basically.

"This is chess with my brother." Janus gave my arm a squeeze. "Tonight, we're making our countermove."

Chess?

So this still *was* a game between them, even with a baby involved?

Suddenly I felt wilted, even in my elegant deep maroon velvet dress that had given me Pretty Woman vibes the moment I'd put it on—except unlike Julia Roberts, I had actual meat on my bones. Curves, Janus called them. He'd then enjoyed manhandling my ass all the way out of the hotel room.

I felt so torn, one second wanting to give in to all the good things they made me feel, and the next... I leaned against a pillar before Janus reached for my arm to pull me into a stream of folks heading in. Since we were coming with just regular press passes instead of with Leander, we weren't heading in down the red carpet. Just in through the back.

Janus didn't seem to have any problem at all not being in the spotlight. Proving his brother had been wrong when he'd accused Janus of being jealous of his stardom? Or he really didn't care? He didn't seem to.

Janus was a complex man, and I didn't understand his motivations any more than his brother's most times. But he seemed excited about the pregnancy and had from the beginning. And God, it did feel good to have his arm in mine guiding me so assuredly up the stairs into the Dubai Arts Center towards the ballroom.

A buzz started up almost the second we arrived in the

ballroom. People flowed in from outside where the movie would be screened, flashbulbs going off constantly, some of which now turned our way. The press had to know Leander was inside already, but the twins appearing together was always a special event.

"Let go of my arm," I said, trying to push off from Janus. "We shouldn't be pictured together." At least not this intimately.

But Janus didn't let go of me. If anything, he kept closer to my side. "You think I'm embarrassed to be seen with you?" He talked through his teeth as he smiled a winning smile to the cameras turning our way.

I was ready to argue with him some more, but by then we'd reached the glittering ballroom. I'd only been to the Met Gala once, last year with Mikayla. This place was equally as fancy as that, if not more.

Everything glittered in golds and creams and whites. Crystal chandeliers twinkled and mood lights were strung throughout. Women everywhere dripped with sparkling jewels that flashed in the light. Men grinned back with perfectly bleached white veneers. This wasn't even a gala, just a movie premiere! Good Lord, these people knew how to party.

My eyes were still searching the room when I saw—

I gulped and stumbled a little. And was more grateful than ever that I was holding Janus's arm.

Because across the room, front and center, were Leander and Lena.

Leander and his gorgeous co-star made a beautiful couple, even I had to admit that as my heart sank through my feet. Leander's arm was wrapped comfortably around

Lena's tiny waist. She, naturally, was angled into him, her hand on his chest, leaning in flirtily.

They were surrounded by press, eating up every second of #Lender.

"I'm not my fuckwit brother." Janus's voice was low in my ear, but hard.

And then he turned towards me, bent me backwards, and kissed me deep.

All around us, flashbulbs went crazy.

I could've stabbed Janus in the face with my kitten heel... except Janus was a really good kisser. I mean, really good. And in spite of all the other craziness, I did have feelings for the big, crazy bastard.

His edges were rougher than Leander's but he lived out loud. He'd wanted me from the beginning. Even the way he'd gone barbarian caveman protector on me the second he'd learned I was pregnant was... well, I couldn't say I wasn't kissing him back within moments.

Janus didn't even know for sure the baby was *his*. Considering the number of times Leander had gone without a condom compared to the once or twice Janus had —it was probably a slim hope.

Then again, it only took once.

I was far from a statistics major in understanding all the probabilities. What was clear, though? Janus was being a stand-up guy. Janus knew how to make my pussy weep in pleasure, and Janus loved me.

Compared to... as soon as Janus set me back upright on my feet, my eyes drifted back towards... hashtag *Lender*.

At least Janus's little trick had created the diversion he

was looking for. Everyone's heads had swung our way—even Leander's.

And the look on his face? Well, let's just say it was less than pleased. I gulped and clung to Janus's hand.

"Who's this with you tonight, Janus?" a reporter with a British accent asked, shoving a microphone towards Janus.

"This is my lovely new fiancée, Hope Robins." Janus grinned and I tried not to choke on my own tongue.

His— His— *what???*

Janus wrapped an arm around my shoulders. "You are looking at the future Mrs. Hope Mavros."

Okay, I was back to wanting to stab him with my heels again.

Or maybe throat punching him.

What the hell did you just do? Yes, I'd come back to the room last night, but that didn't mean I— I mean, we hadn't even had time to discuss things! We'd all blown up at each other, then Leander had tied me up and we'd slept! We hadn't talked about the future, or expectations, or—!

But of course, we were in front of cameras, so all I could do was stand there, clutch Janus's arm, and grin like my life depended on it. Oh, and try to tamp down the urge to hurl the sleeve of crackers I'd managed to finally eat back at the hotel right in front of these reporters' feet!

"How long have you two known each other?" came a shouted voice.

And then another, "Does Leander approve?"

I almost choked on my tongue on that one. Janus just smiled enigmatically and responded, "I'm not my brother's keeper and he's not mine. Next question!"

Leander never came near, even though we were answering questions until right before the movie started.

And he was trapped during the movie, forced to sit up front with Lena and the rest of his stars, since he hadn't planned to come with his brother. Janus sat me between Milo and himself. I was glad I'd seen the movie before, because his hand alternately was massaging my knee and curled around my shoulder. Unlike the last premiere we'd attended, even though it was dark in the theater, this time I could tell many eyes were on us. Even though theoretically we were here to celebrate Leander.

I guess, thinking about it... I never had seen anything in the tabloids about Janus dating anyone. Not seriously, anyway. He'd be pictured with women occasionally, but never the same one twice.

And he'd essentially just proposed in front of a live crowd.

"What were you thinking?" I hissed in his ear the second I could pull him away from the crowd.

Janus's eyes were intense and serious as he looked down at me. Flashes popped and I knew we couldn't talk long because reporters were watching, capturing every moment of our whispered conversation. "I'm just cutting to the chase."

He leaned his head down so no one could read his lips. "That's our baby. This is forever. I'm making it official."

I pulled back and could only blink up wide-eyed at him. "But we've only— I mean, and he—" I looked around for Leander, only to see him glance our direction, look away, and disappear through a doorway.

"Screw him," Janus said fervently, grabbing my attention back. "Do you love me?"

I blinked, my heart beating as fast as a rabbit's. A gorgeous man stood in front of me, one I loved, and he reached out to clutch my hand. I nodded.

He leaned his head down so our foreheads touched, and it was like no one else was in the room. "Then say it out loud, honey."

"I l-l-love you," I whispered, my breath hitching.

A smile like sunshine breaking after a storm broke on his face. "Then we have everything I ever dreamed of. Will you marry me?"

Shakily, I nodded. And whispered. "Yes."

He leaned down and kissed me. I sank against him as flashbulbs exploded all around us.

THREE

HOPE

WE DIDN'T SEE LEANDER the rest of the night, and frankly at this point, good riddance. I rested my head against Janus's chest on the ride home as he plucked pins out of my hair and Milo massaged my feet.

I was in heaven. As much as a bloated, achy, tired, jet-lagged pregnant woman could be.

The ride was too short, and then I had to put my devil heels back on for the walk back up to our suite.

But as soon as we there, Janus made an executive order. "Bath time. Now."

I wanted to whine that I just wanted to go to bed. But Janus wasn't having it.

"Baby, we just announced to the world that we're going to be man and wife," Janus said as they sat me down on the bed. Milo immediately dropped to the ground and undid my shoes again, massaging as he pulled them off my feet.

I could only blink up at him. In spite of all he'd said at the gala... "Wasn't that just some publicity stunt? Or to get back at Leander?"

Janus looked offended. He got in my space, pushing me back on the bed, his weight on top of me. "I don't do those kinds of stunts, babe. I mean what I say. Always. Were you stuntin' when you said you loved me?"

I swallowed, his face inches from mine, his body heavy and so amazingly solid on top of mine. He wasn't squashing me; he just made me feel so wonderfully *female*. And seen. He made me feel seen and loved and important. I'd felt like a wall-flower forever, just blending in invisibly to the background.

"You want to marry me?" I breathed out in shock.

"I want to marry you, and for you to have this baby, and then a passel more. I want to plant my seed deep in you every night."

I blinked, confused. "But what about..." My eyes went over Janus's shoulder to where Milo stood watching.

"Milo's always welcome. Leander's welcome too if he ever gets his head outta his ass." He leaned down, pressing his body further into mine, his groin mashing against mine. "But it'll be *my name* on the marriage license. Because I recognized your value and worth first."

My heart, body, and soul melted for him.

I was liquid as he slid back off the bed and pulled me with him. I groaned. I'd been perfectly happy where we were.

But considering he got me to my feet only so Milo could unzip my dress and peel it from my body, well...

After my dress was a maroon pool at my feet along with

my underclothes, they led me to the bathroom. Our suite had both a shower and a huge, multi-jet jacuzzi bath. I had to admit, I love the ways these guys traveled. And how they manhandled me, helping me from both sides to climb up the steps and down into the water that Milo had started as soon as we'd come in, apparently.

"Oh God, that feels good," I breathed out.

"That's right, honey," Janus said, "let it all go."

Damn, those were the magic words. I felt my muscles unclenching from tension I hadn't even realized I was holding.

Milo came near with makeup wipes and gently swiped my face clean. I laid back while he and Janus washed my body and hair.

I couldn't describe how luxurious it was to be washed by someone other than myself. It felt like I was the richest woman in the world, or Cleopatra in an era long past being worshipped in a bathhouse. I went limp as their hands moved up and down me.

And I'd never felt safer as I gave myself over to them. Gave away all my worries and anxieties and sadness and fears. They carried it away as they washed the shampoo out of my hair and scrubbed my scalp.

Then when Janus's firm hands massaged up my thighs, I spread for him, my legs flopping limply open wide. The water sloshed with the motion and Janus smiled. "That's my good, good girl," he murmured.

There was soft music playing in the background and I didn't even know when they'd turned it on. They'd blissed me out so hard.

And that was before Janus's thick finger started toying with my sex.

He didn't immediately start pushing, he just rubbed, massaging in the same motions he'd been rubbing my legs. But where he put pressure...

I groaned and dropped my head against the sloped back of the tub. Milo had put a folded towel there as a little pillow.

"Look at our beautiful girl," Milo whispered. "So wet and glistening."

"She's been such a good girl all night," Janus answered him. "How about we give our good girl a reward?"

"You touching her pussy?"

"Oh yeah. She's all puffy for me."

I groaned and pressed up against him. He was right. I hadn't realized but their touching had been raising desire in me. It had all been so hazy. Damn, they'd been tricking me by lulling me into this amazing dream space, and now they were going to ramp up the pleasure?

"Oh God," I hissed, my eyes closed as I leaned further into Janus's touch. He wasn't even entering me with his finger, just putting pressure against my entire sex.

"Her nipples are getting so hard," Milo breathed out.

"You thinking about what it'll feel like to get your dick in her?" Janus asked, adding pressure so that his fingers were pushing into the soft fleshy cavity towards my anus, then back towards my pussy—

A high-pitched whine slipped from my throat as I started coming.

He palmed my pussy like he owned it. Because he would. The man I was going to marry.

I thrust against him, losing all control. Water splashed and Janus's thick, veined arm disappearing into the water was the hottest thing I'd seen as my eyes popped open.

He palmed my pussy, first against my clit, then the flat fingers of his hand massaging round and round at my opening.

I whined, feeling my emptiness so acutely because I was used to being stuffed full. "Please," I begged.

"Please what?" Milo's voice had a frenetic edge. "What do you want? Do you want his fingers up your cunt? Do you want him to finger-fuck you?"

"Yes!"

"Then beg me, baby," Janus growled.

"Finger-fuck me," I cried.

"Where?" Janus asked. "Where do you want these fingers?"

I spasmed at the question. "Wherever you want them, Daddy."

"That's the right answer, Princess."

And then a finger slipped inside me as Janus's other hand thrust into the water. His finger inside me curved backwards like a come-hither motion, hooking some place inside me that—

I screamed and no one tried to stop me. So I grabbed part of the towel and shoved it in my own mouth.

Especially when the fingers of Janus's other hand started pushing at my other puckered hole.

Meanwhile, at my pussy, a second finger pushed for entry together with the first. I writhed in the water.

"Look at our little siren squirm," Milo said, wiping my wet hair from my face. "I was so hard all through the movie.

She was a goddamn wet dream in that dress. Her ass... Jesus *fuck.*"

"I know," Janus said low and dark. "I needed to feel this little pussy. Fuck, why haven't I ever put my hands in you before?"

His fingers at my anus massaged hard, spreading me as he sought entrance. I was used to being penetrated there, but still.

"Just when you think her skin is the softest thing about her," Janus growled. His fingers at my anus pushed in and in. How could his fingers feel thicker than their cocks?

"How many fingers do you have back there?" I gasped.

"Three," Janus grinned, and then kept pushing. "The water is keeping you ready and wet. You can take it. I'm gonna fist you back here, baby."

I whined and squirmed in the water, splashing it over the edge. "I don't think I can take it."

"Try," Janus commanded, three fingers back there squeezing and opening as they pushed for entrance. "You're gonna take my fist up your ass so pretty, baby. I know you can. Gonna take it easy on your pussy for a while but that doesn't mean your ass is getting any time off."

"Jesus fuck, watch her face as she stretches for you," Milo breathed out, and I could hear the rhythmic slapping of his hand running harshly up and down his shaft. When I looked over at him, I saw he'd used some of my shampoo as lotion. These filthy, fucked-up men.

I flipped around in the water as Janus bent over, half in the bathwater now as he massaged me and his fingers kept thrusting in my ass.

And I came as his fingertips breached the ring of muscle at my anus.

Right as Leander slammed the bathroom door open, looking furious.

"Anyone wanna tell me what the *fuck* is going on here?"

FOUR

HOPE

"I'M FUCKING MY FIANCÉE, OBVIOUSLY," Janus said calmly, not letting his hands up from my ass or pussy. "That's what's going on."

I could only writhe in the water. Leander's fury just made me come harder. He'd abandoned me but Janus loved me. So maybe I was putting on a little extra performance.

Or maybe Janus and Milo were simply making me come so hard there was nothing else to do but—

I screamed into the towel again, my eyes all but rolling backwards in my head.

"Get your hands off her," Leander roared. "We have rules! I said to keep her tied to the fucking bed."

Janus kept finger-fucking me, working his three fingers deeper in my ass. "Rules?" he said sarcastically. "Yeah, like we discuss shit before making decisions? You threw out the rule book first, bro. Seems to me we get to make our own rules from here on out."

It was not the right thing to say to Leander at that moment but considering the way Janus was pleasuring me out of my goddamned mind, I couldn't exactly be the reasonable one and deescalate the situation. Plus... I agreed with Janus. Leander was an asshole and— oh, oh, *oh*—

"Get your hands out of my fucking woman!" Leander roared.

"Your woman?" Janus laughed, hands working me even harder. His undershirt was soaked with water and it splashed out of the bathtub onto the floor as he manhandled my body. "She's *my* fiancée. If anyone's outta line here, seems like it's you, bro. You sure seemed cozy with Lena tonight. Hashtag *Lender* trending?"

"No, you fuck. The only thing anyone could ask me about was *you* and the mysterious woman you'd suddenly declared you were engaged to. How the fuck do you think this looks? I'm trying to fly under the radar and you pull this fucking stunt?"

Janus froze, his jovial mask slipping before he picked up his sensual torture again. "Because everything's about *you*, isn't it, brother? I couldn't *possibly* be thinking about the woman who's having our baby. I couldn't possibly be thinking about my *own* future and happiness for once, could I?"

Leander stood there fuming.

Meanwhile, I writhed in the tub, gasping for air and coming, and, oh *God*—

Janus was rotating the fingers in my ass. He flattened them and he was rotating long fingers back and forth as he pushed in and out. Meanwhile, his hand deep in my pussy pressed against a spot so far inside—at the same time as he thrust in with his three fingers up my ass—

"*Oh God!!!*" I cried.

"See how happy I make her?" Janus addressed his brother, who still stood with his arms crossed in the door-way, emitting fury like a cloud. "I make her come harder and longer than you ever could. You aren't the boss of any of us."

Leander looked like his gasket was about to blow.

Instead, he just gritted out through clenched teeth, "Just keep your cock out of that pussy. No one fucks her cunt again until *my* doctor checks her out."

He glared at us all. "And finish the fuck up. The reason I didn't ream your ass out for disobedience at the premiere was because I was locking up a backroom deal. Considering I just inked a four-month contract for my next movie and I write checks to every fucking one of you, *yes,* I actually am the boss of you. I'm the new Jason Steele. Filming starts in Venice next week. We need to get our asses on a flight in about"—he looked at the expensive watch on his wrist—"two hours."

"But Henry Cavill got that part," Janus said, his hands on me pausing.

"He dropped out due to an injury. So why don't you get your hands out of her cunt and get fucking packing so you can do your damn job. Or am I the only one concerned with earning a goddamned paycheck around here?"

With that, Leander roughly yanked at the knot of his tie and slammed the bathroom door shut behind him.

I collapsed, sinking all the way underneath the water

until my body was entirely submerged and my hair floated above me.

It was peaceful under here, quiet. And I could feel the residual pleasure Janus had brought me to over and over again resounding in my body, echoing throughout the water and back.

My peace was short-lived, though, because soon enough strong arms were reaching down and hauling me out of the water and onto the fluffy mat outside the tub. I stood shakily while Janus swiped my sopping hair out of my face.

"Don't let that asshole get to you. You and me can march outta here any time you want. We don't have to stay. I won't let you be disrespected like that."

I blinked up at him, which was easier once Milo handed me a towel to wipe my face. Did he really mean that? So it *was* about more than just one-upping his brother? "You would do that? Leave?" I whispered.

"No brainer," Janus said, dropping a hand down to my belly. "Babe. We're a family now."

It meant everything to hear him say that. But I couldn't rip him away from his brother. He'd stood by Leander all these years.

So I managed a smile as Milo helped wrap my wet hair. "I'm fine. As long as you two are by my side," I reached out dripping hands towards both Milo and Janus, "I'll be just fine."

A grin exploded across Janus's face and he leaned down to press a kiss to my forehead. Then he helped Milo enthusiastically dry me off and wrap me in a towel.

Just when I'd started to relax, the door banged open again, and Leander was back. It was clear from his pinched features that he was still pissed. "You know, I can't believe I'm getting this kind of fucking disrespect from you, brother, when I went out of my way for you on this one. There're lots of stunts and I got you on the contract as one of my doubles."

Janus put his arm protectively around my shoulders and I clutched my towel tighter. "Getting to pretend to be you?" Janus rolled his eyes. "What a fucking honor."

"On camera, you dipshit. Earning your own paycheck for once in your life instead of just living off my talent."

Since Janus's arm was around me, I could feel him tense up in anger at his brother's words.

"Plus, it's the kind of shit you love." Leander tossed a hand out, rolling his eyes impatiently. "Driving fast cars. Jumping off buildings. Even riding a goddamn horse for one scene. You're tired of living in the background and I'm giving you a chance to do what you love."

Janus's fingers clamped tighter around my shoulder. "Or you're trying to keep me away from *her*."

Leander's eyes flicked my way but only briefly. It was like he couldn't even look at me ever since I'd revealed I was pregnant. It hurt and pissed me off all at the same time.

"Maybe we could all use some breathing space," Leander said. And before Janus could react with the angry retort I could feel in his body language, Leander continued, "Even Hope. Look at her. She's pregnant and exhausted. At least with my plan she'd get some rest without you breathing down her cunt every second."

"Yeah, cause being tied to a bed is *so* restful," Janus said sarcastically.

"Do you want the job or not?" Leander bit back.

Janus's arm around me squeezed and then relaxed as he breathed out. "Staying all together is still probably the best plan. For the moment, anyway." Then he turned to face me. "You okay with going to Italy, babe?"

I was taken aback and touched at being asked. My own desires were so rarely, if ever, taken into consideration. I glowed at his care.

Until Leander butted in, that was. "She's the publicist," he snapped. "Of course she's coming."

"Don't be an asshole," Milo said shortly, and Leander looked surprised to be getting it from him too. But I smiled, warm from the two of them defending me. Leander needed to clue in that everyone could see his asshole-ish behavior from a mile away. Everyone except him, that was.

Leander just grabbed the door and backed away, glaring at all of us. "I don't see anyone packing. It's an hour forty-five till we leave now. If you're not ready by the time I am, you can find your own damn ride to Venice."

FIVE

HOPE

WHILE THE FILM would be shot in Venice, we were staying in nearby Padua, a little bit inland, on dry land. The boys were training the first month anyway.

I'd been a little disappointed when Milo explained their schedule to me on the way here, but when we arrived in Padua, my mind immediately changed.

The city felt like it had been transported from another time. All the buildings were beautiful burnt-orange terracotta, cream stucco, and brick. The streets were cobbled and ancient tiles. It felt magical. Colorful market stalls and porticos exploded with fresh fruits, pastries, and every delicious food you could imagine.

If only I didn't feel like barfing every other minute.

It was a true tragedy to be in the country with the best food in the world and all I could manage to get down for most of the day was a few bites of bread and then *maybe* in the afternoon some tomato soup.

Granted, it was the best tomato soup I'd *ever* eaten in my life. While Janus and Leander disappeared every morning, I slept in—I was *so* sleepy lately!—then dragged my achy body out of bed somewhere around noon.

Milo had breakfast waiting for me, usually just some toasted ciabatta slices. Then I'd make my way out onto the sunny balcony to watch the bustling city while I tried to get the food down. Then I'd get started on what was always an overwhelming amount of email.

Leander's last movie *Trapdoor* was still making big numbers at the box office over a month after release and Hollywood was realizing he was the new It Guy. So everyone wanted him for their new project. So many scripts and project offers were coming in, along with requests for interviews and appearances, Milo and I were kept just as busy as the twins.

Leander had gotten his way—when didn't he?—and I'd visited a doctor of his choosing the second week after we'd arrived. At least she'd been a kindly Italian woman who spoke excellent English. She'd made me feel at ease as she led me through a few non-invasive tests and let me hear the baby's heartbeat for the first time.

I sobbed at hearing proof of the little creature inside me. It made it feel far more real. I'd refused to let anyone in the appointment with me—my own little rebellion at Leander's controlling nature. The nurse made a recording of the heartbeat for the twins to listen to later since they couldn't take the day off training.

From the dates of my last period cycle, the doctor gave

us a likely window of conception dates. Milo was there with me, plus the doctor gave me her notes in a report for Leander.

He read it that night with a furrow in his brow before Janus yanked the paper out of his hand. Janus's eyes scanned the paper quickly and then a grin broke out on his face.

"Ha!" Janus said. "The doc says she got knocked up right after she first started working for us. It could have been that first time we fucked on the plane before she even started the pill. So either of us could be the father."

Janus pulled me close and cupped my cheeks. "Our baby could be *mine*." He grinned down at me like I was everything in the world to him.

"Or not," Leander snapped. "She could have lied about being a virgin and been knocked up before she ever started working for us."

Janus let go of my cheeks and spun to look at his brother, standing between me and him like a shield. "Fuck off. You felt her. She was a goddamned virgin and you can get the fuck out of here if you're going to talk to the mother of my child like that."

Leander scoffed. "There's every chance that's my baby in there. *Way* more chances, in fact."

"Well, at least you're admitting it," Milo said softly from behind me.

Leander spun on his friend like he was part of a mutiny, then headed for the door. "I'm hitting the weight room. And if you don't want to lose the job as my double, brother, you better join me so your muscles keep up with mine."

He slammed out the door of the apartment the studio

had put us up in. Janus had given me a squeeze. "Such exciting news, honey," and then he'd gone off to join his brother.

And so it went. Leander didn't sleep with us anymore. He took a bed in one of the other rooms in the four-bedroom apartment while Janus and Milo snuggled up with me each night. I was most often nauseated again at night, so there wasn't a lot of funny business going on, just them sandwiching me as we all snuggled up to sleep. Apart from a few hours in the afternoon where the nausea let up, I was usually curled up and glad I could work from bed.

A little more than five weeks after we'd gotten there, Milo was out getting groceries and the nausea was manageable. I was out on the balcony doing some work, when I set down my laptop and looked out on the city.

I was in one of the most amazing, historic countries in the world and I'd been tucked up in this stupid apartment. I looked around and put a hand on the beautiful, tiled balcony. *Sorry, apartment, you're gorgeous, I didn't mean it.* It really was one of the most beautiful places I'd ever stayed. I just had a hella case of cabin fever.

I put a hand on my tummy. I'd had no clue pregnancy could be this wretched. *Never again*, I swore. It must have been men who'd named it *morning* sickness. Trying to trick us women into having their spawn. Because it was *all day* sickness, truth be told!

Okay, enough. I was done with being stuck in this apartment and seeing this gorgeous city from three stories up. I didn't care how beautiful the view was.

I went to the closet and hunted for my shoes. Outside shoes, that is. I'd barely unpacked them, so I really had to root them out. And, I frowned, why the hell had I packed so many damn heels? Yes, I had been thinking of premieres and press events and not Lamaze classes, but still...!

I groaned as I pulled out yet another pair of heels and threw them towards the back of the closet into the shadows. Really, I wanted to throw them in the trash. I was cursing Mikayla for her *no Doc Martens* rule, cause I could really use some ankle support right about now.

Ah! There! At the bottom of my bag were some Keds and I hugged them to my chest before grabbing socks and then slipping them on my feet.

Or trying to. What the hell? These usually slipped on fine. But now I had to untie them, and even then, they barely fit. I blinked. I'd read in the pregnancy book that pregnant women's feet could get bigger, but I was a bit horrified to see the real-life evidence.

I was going to need a whole new wardrobe pretty soon. I was starting to feel a tightness across my abdomen now that I was almost officially three months preggers. At some point, this would sink in as real, right? More than just in brief moments like at the ultrasound listening to the heartbeat.

I tied the tight shoes the rest of the way, shucked off my sweatshirt and pulled on a nice sundress. Then I grabbed my purse, wrote a quick note for Milo that I was taking a walk, and headed out.

Jogging down the stairs, I felt my heart lighten. I did yoga in the apartment to try to keep limber and do *something* active, but it felt good to use all my limbs.

And when I burst out of the door into the bright, sunny streets, I felt a burden lift from my chest I hadn't even realized was there.

I breathed the fresh air in deep. Padua was close enough to the sea that I could smell it on the air, along with... I sniffed and God, something smelled delicious.

It was such a novel sensation—for food to smell...*good*, instead of sending me running for the toilet.

So I followed my nose. And it led me down a narrow cobblestone street with terracotta buildings towering three stories on either side, until it opened onto a large piazza, the one I could see from my balcony.

I smiled as I walked out into the sunlight and wandered among the stalls. Everything looked better than the last. But when I came across a little shop, a hole in the wall selling pizza, well, I figured why not start with the classics?

Pizza in Italy? Um, yes, please.

Janus and Leander were on a strict training diet, and Milo had taken to eating outside the apartment since there were a couple weeks I couldn't even stand the *smell* of meat within a ten-foot radius.

The shop owner, a man in his fifties with graying hair that stuck out like Einstein's, just kept grinning at me and saying, "È delizioso! Buon appetite!" as he handed over the slice.

The cheese was bubbled over and the bread looked so fresh. My stomach rumbled. "Grazie, grazie!" I said as I handed over some euros and took the pizza. A flood of Italian came my way as he grinned back at me.

I just lifted the pizza again and repeated, "Grazie!"

Then I found a spot on the side of a big fountain in the center of the sunlit plaza where I could sit. A few kids played nearby, running around and laughing their little heads off. It made my heart squeeze in a way it never had before.

I'd never thought much about kids, other than swearing I was never gonna be like my Mama, tied to the nursery and the kitchen.

I always threw myself into my work instead. I loved being a working woman. Traveling the world had always thrilled me. And what would happen to me now? What would happen once I gave birth to this baby?

I'd been living in a sort of stasis up in that apartment, denying the reality of time marching forward and all that meant.

Well, maybe I could keep denying for a little while longer. It was my specialty, right? And at the moment I had a little slice of heaven on a paper plate in my hands. I lifted the piece of hot prosciutto pizza high, mozzarella strings dripping, and took my first bite—

I moaned loud enough that a couple nearby looked my way. I couldn't care.

Dear holy baby Jesus in a manger, that salty cheese! And the crust! It all melted in my mouth in a cheesy, salty—

I chewed and then shoved another bite in my mouth. Cheese dripped down my chin and I didn't care. I muffled my groan this time but let my head fall back as I chewed the most delicious pizza on God's green earth.

Then I hit a bite with prosciutto. And holy—

It wasn't just salty processed meat like I was used to— there were so many flavors in that one little slice of heaven.

I took another bite, and another. And my stomach didn't revolt. In fact, I'd never felt hungrier. After I finished the slice, devouring the soft, luscious crust and licking the oil from my fingers, I closed my eyes and sat basking in the sun.

For one brief but solid moment, I felt at peace all the way down to my center.

"Jesus, I've been looking for you everywhere!"

I frowned as my sun was blocked and I opened my eyes.

Milo was standing over me, and he did not look happy. "What were you thinking, leaving the apartment alone?"

I frowned and sat up, putting my plate on the tile beside me. "I told you in the note. I'm out for a walk. I didn't think I was a prisoner."

Milo breathed out hard. "You aren't. But still, you should have one of us with you."

Considering I'd just felt the first bit of peace in forever, he was pissing me off. "So you *are* my warden?"

"Fuck, Hope, no, that's not what I meant." He huffed out a breath as he picked up the empty plate and sat down beside me. Then he did a double-take at the plate. "You ate?"

"I was feeling good so I decided to take a walk." I narrowed my eyes at him. "Which I am perfectly free to do anytime I damn please."

He held his hands up. "Okay, but why not take me with you?"

"Sometimes maybe I need some space!" I exploded. "All of this—" I gestured around but then my hand fell to my stomach and I lost some of my steam. He was bringing me back to reality and I wasn't sure I was ready for that. "It's a lot sometimes, okay? I'm gonna need space to myself."

He frowned. "Janus and Leander won't like it."

"Well, maybe I don't always give a fuck what they like or don't like," I said vehemently.

Milo's eyebrows went up at me, cursing. I was usually such a good little girl for them. Well, screw that. They would all run roughshod over me if I didn't stand up for what I wanted. What I needed.

"They're just protective," he said, quieter. "We all are."

I harrumphed and didn't give him a response. Instead, I looked away from him and people watched the hubbub around the piazza.

He was quiet for a time and that was fine by me. I was happy to just drink in the sunshine.

"Did I ever tell you how we all met?" Milo asked, surprising me. None of them ever talked about the past, so I'd taken it as off limits.

I turned to look at him. "You met on the set of *Who's Counting Now?*, right?"

He nodded. "I was older than them. On the show I was just the neighbor kid who'd come over sometimes to babysit. Comic relief."

"You were good."

He laughed and made a face. "No, I wasn't."

"For a kid, you were."

He shrugged. "Sure, I could spit back lines and ham it up a little for the cameras, but it was never gonna go beyond kid tv show stuff. I was fine with that."

"So you all got to be friends, right? And then your mom adopted them when their parents died?"

He looked at me sideways. "That was the story Mom spun for the tabloids, sure. But I was nine, and they were four. We were hardly friends. I thought they were annoying. But Mom was the ultimate stage mom. And she saw the writing on the wall with me. I was getting tall and awkward, aging out of the prime kid star roles. She loved being on set, even on days I didn't have scenes. She'd help out with the twins in between scenes, so no one complained about it.

"It helped her case when she petitioned for custody after their parents died. There was no one else. Just one grandparent so old he had to be on oxygen all the time—hardly a candidate to chase after two rambunctious four-year-old boys. And there was my mom, ready, willing, and swearing she already loved the boys and they loved her."

I blinked, totally immersed in the story he was telling. This was nothing like the sanitary publicized version of events.

"So they gave them to her, just like that?"

Milo shrugged. "It was Hollywood in the late nineties. There was plenty of B-roll of the twins with Mom. And she could put on such a good show in public."

My stomach soured. "A good show?"

He nodded and met my eyes. "Narcissists are good at that. Putting on a good face for the public, ya know. Really, she just saw the opportunity to have genuine *stars* as sons. They were young enough she could mold them just the way she wanted, she thought. The mistakes she'd made with me —not getting me in the biz early enough, not pushing hard enough—she could fix with them. Plus, as she told me repeatedly, they were cuter than I ever was. They had real *potential*."

"Jesus," I breathed out, putting a hand on Milo's arm. He shrugged like it didn't mean anything, but I could tell it had hurt him, his mother's rejection in favor of the twins.

"I'm so sorry. I've met those kinds of stage moms. They're the worst. What'd your dad say about it?"

He laughed harshly. "Dad? He divorced her and split not long after. He'd never wanted kids in the first place, much less a pair of four-year-old twins that weren't his."

"Jesus," I said again.

"Yeah." Milo looked out at the piazza, a faraway look in his eyes.

"Why are you telling me all this, Milo?"

He turned his head back to me, eyes focusing in. "'Cause it fucked both of them up in different ways when it comes to family. Being wanted, but not for themselves. Then with the kid thing..." He looked towards my stomach.

"What? What about the *kid thing*?"

He hesitated, then came out with it. "Leander swore he'd never have kids, 'cause he always said he'd never fuck up any kids the way we were fucked up."

I breathed out heavily. Well, damn. "Then why the hell was he even playing around with the day-after pill? If he feels like that?"

Milo looked at me like it was obvious. "Because it was *you*. Before, he was always religious about using condoms with every other woman. Except for you." He looked out again. "And then there's Janus."

I frowned. "What about Janus?"

Dear Lord, I wasn't sure how much more bad news I could handle. One of the potential fathers of my unborn child didn't want kids. Awesome. And the other?

"Well, he's the exact opposite," Milo said. "He always wanted family, in a major way. Since Leander and me were all he had, he stuck with us like glue. But we both knew he always wanted more. Kids, a wife, white picket fence, the whole shebang. It's always been a hole in his life."

I swallowed hard and blinked.

"You're everything Janus has always wanted and Leander knows it. It's freaking him out in addition to everything else."

"None of that is my fault!" I said.

Milo turned to me again, compassion on his face. "I know, but it's still the reality of the situation."

I threw my head back again, my brain spinning with all this new information. Then I sat up straight again and looked at Milo. "What about *you*? What do you want in all this? You just keep talking about Leander and Janus."

Milo looked surprised. "Oh, me? I'm fine. I just go along with whatever—"

But I shook my head and held up a hand. "That's bullshit. You just sat here and dissected the twins' motives. You know them better than anyone because you've devoted your whole life to them. Why? You said it yourself. You didn't even like them in the beginning."

"Well, that was then," Milo said, brushing me off. "We had a five-year age difference. It changed as we grew up."

I frowned. There was a lot he was still sweeping under the rug. He'd said his mom was a narcissist but had left it at that. There had to be a ton more to it.

In my business, I'd met plenty of narcissists, and avoided them whenever I came into contact with one. You started to recognize the signals after a while, though sometimes it took time because they were often so good at appearing like your best friend at first. *Love-bombing*, I'd learned was the technical term.

But once they had you under their spell, it all changed. They took you for granted and then the abuse started. They could cut you down and make you feel about as big as an ant in three seconds flat. Only those closest to them saw the *real* version of them. Everyone else got to see the lovable, charismatic side.

I should know. I'd grown up with one.

My father.

Everyone in our congregation loved him. Each Sunday of my whole life, I'd been told what a lucky girl I was to have him as a dad.

What a lucky, lucky girl.

The couple times I'd tried to tell anyone about the rages he could go into, the way he shouted verbal abuse at me and my mother, how he broke us down every day until we were nothing...

Well, they'd told my father on me, sure I was "acting out." And for a lot of my life I thought they were right—that *I* was the one in the wrong. The bad girl. The one who deserved all the harsh punishments he meted out.

I reached out and grasped Milo's wrist. "It's not your fault, you know."

Milo looked up at me, confused.

"What she did to them. And to you. None of it's your fault."

Milo blinked several times, then swallowed hard and looked at the cobblestones at our feet. He didn't nod but shrugged noncommittally. "I was older and I knew what she was like. I should've protected them better."

My heart broke for him as I shook my head. "You were

just a kid too. You weren't supposed to be the adult. *She* was."

He shrugged again, and I could tell he wasn't taking in what I was saying. He couldn't, probably. Narcissists programmed their children from such a young age to take the blame they refused to accept themselves. They were perpetual victims, even at the expense of their children. It was *our* fault, they claimed—and it took us until we were adults to realize that was total bullshit. That a little child couldn't be at fault when the *adult* was supposed to be the responsible, grown-up one.

"We were all just kids," I whispered, and Milo looked up at me sharply.

"We?"

I'd showed too much of my hand and I stood up abruptly. "I've been in the sun too long. Why don't we head back to the apartment?"

"Hope," Milo started but I just grabbed his hand with one of mine.

"Let's go home," I said, trying to shove away all unpleasant thoughts and recapture the day. I smiled saucily at him. "I think I'm feeling up to a bath." I lifted my eyebrows. "That is, if you're up to helping me bathe?"

He grinned back at me. "Always at your service, beautiful."

"And maybe," I took his hand as we started to walk back, tossing my plate in a waste bin as we passed, "you and me could take walks in the afternoon now that I'm feeling better? Maybe you could show me the city?"

He squeezed my hand. "It would be my honor."

SIX

HOPE

"WHAT THE HELL?" Janus said as he came in the door.

I gasped and looked up from the couch... where Milo was bent between my legs eating me out.

"That's what I'm always fuckin' saying," Leander laughed, pushing in behind Janus. "Now you know what it feels like."

Milo just looked over his shoulder at them both, making no move to swipe at his chin that glistened with my juices. As soon as we'd gotten home from my impromptu walk, he'd pushed me down on the couch and tossed my dress up.

And his mouth felt—oh God, I'd forgotten how good it was to be eaten out. I always thought it couldn't possibly feel this amazing. Then I was reminded every time any of them put their mouth on me.

But Milo was an especially giving lover in this way.

"What are you waiting for, then?" Milo asked Janus before turning back to me, his eyes bright. "You can join in."

He grasped the tops of my thighs and dipped his head back to my sex, blowing warm air even as he pried my puffy sex apart with his thumbs.

I shivered and my eyes rolled back in my head.

"Goddamn," Janus said, immediately grabbing his shirt in the back and shucking it off over his head in one motion, along with his undershirt.

Leander just stood there indecisively on the threshold even as Janus came towards us with a grin.

"You feelin' better, baby?" Janus asked as he dipped a knee down on the couch beside where I was writhing. Because, oh God, Milo's lips had suckered around my engorged clit, his tongue flicking back and forth, and back and forth—

I reached out a hand and dug it into the back of Janus's hair desperately as soon as he got close enough. "Kiss me?" I begged.

"You never have to ask twice," he said huskily and bent over to kiss me deep. Devouring me.

"What?" Leander said from where he stood near the door, crossing his arms. "Am I the only rational human being left here? We just got home. We haven't had dinner yet."

Janus pulled away from my kiss only long enough to grin back at his brother. "If you ask nicely, I'm sure Milo will let you have a turn so you can eat too."

Leander's eyes flared and I wasn't sure if it was with fury or interest at his brother's proposal. Hell, maybe it was a mix of both.

"Oh, grow up," Leander said, then stormed off in the direction of the kitchen.

Janus laughed and bent down for another kiss, while at the same time he reached to tweak my exposed nipples.

If only Leander could get over his crap, we might have a real chance at this. Things with Janus and Milo were so excellent. And sure, Milo had explained a little of what was behind Leander's mood...but Janus had lost his parents too, and he wasn't always acting like a little—

"Seven a.m. call time tomorrow," Leander snapped towards Janus before disappearing around the corner into the kitchen. He'd kept his eyes averted from my nakedness apart from his initial shocked gaze. "Don't be late."

Fine by me. Either he pulled his head out of his ass or he didn't.

When I'd first learned about the pregnancy, I'd felt so overwhelmed and lost. But I was stronger now. I was determined to raise this baby right. No matter what. The last month had been good for that, at least. Even if I had to do it all by myself, this baby would feel loved and wanted. I'd prefer to give them a father, but not if I didn't think my guys weren't up to the job. Harsh, perhaps, but true.

With me and Leander skating on thin fucking ice... I'd decided to put off any decision making until a month or two before the baby was born, though.

So far Janus and Milo had been stepping up with each opportunity that I gave them. Leander on the other hand... I watched his retreating back and wished him good riddance.

Janus distracted me with another kiss.

I'd missed his mouth on mine. And Milo's. And their

hands. I writhed as Milo clenched my thighs and went back to my clit.

And then Leander banged back through the door from the kitchen. I looked up in surprise and so did Janus. Milo couldn't be distracted, though—if anything, he only focused in harder.

"You know what, no. She's just as much mine as either of yours." He came back and sat down opposite Janus on my other side.

"She's not a possession," Janus growled, but Leander ignored him.

"Look," he said as he sat down, his thigh touching mine as he actually looked me in the eye for once. Usually he spoke to the room, or over my head addressing only Janus or Milo. But now he was talking right to me.

"I wanna fuck you." He said it direct, no frills. "I'm horny and I wanna fuck. Till we figure out what's going on here and if that's my baby, I'm not fucking anyone else. So can I stick my dick in you?"

I blinked at him, my hips jutting up into Milo's face as another burst of pleasure hit. I could barely concentrate on what Leander was saying, though I could feel it was important. He wanted to fuck me. "But it won't mean anything to you. That's what you're saying."

"Exactly." Leander nodded concisely.

"Fuck off," Janus started but Milo finally lifted his head. He swiped his mouth with his forearm and met my eyes. "It's up to Hope."

I blinked down at him between my legs, my chest heaving from all the pleasure peaks he'd been bringing me to over and over. After our talk earlier and spending so much time with him while the twins were away, I felt a special connection with Milo. I trusted his instincts.

So I looked back to Leander and stared into his blue-gray eyes that took on the color of his shirt. And I saw the boy Milo had described earlier in the man standing before me now. A man who had sworn he'd never have kids because he was terrified of damaging them the way he'd been damaged. I understood the place of fear and deep hurt that came from.

So regardless of the wisdom or lack thereof, I held out my hand to Leander. He strode forward but then it was Janus holding a hand up.

"Not so fast," Janus said. "You don't call the shots anymore. You answer to my rules."

Leander rolled his eyes but I shot him a look. "You want in, you listen to him."

Janus squeezed my love handles. He had this habit of clutching me right in my squishy bits—in other words, he treated my love handles like love handles. I'd tried to push his hands away the first few times, whispering that women didn't like to acknowledge those bits. And he said they were his favorite parts of me, in addition to... then he squeezed my ass.

Which he also grabbed now as he hauled me onto his lap and then flipped me over so I was on my knees.

"Oh!" I gasped, lurching forward over Janus' lap, my elbows landing on the arm of the couch.

"Gentle with her," Milo said.

"I talked to the doctor," Janus said. "He said sex and regular exercise should be fine. And anal sex won't bother the baby at all." Janus walloped my ass.

I shuddered.

"I ordered something and it finally came in today, baby," Janus said.

"Stop fucking talking and put it on her, I saw you open the fucking box at the gym."

"I told you I was in charge tonight," Janus growled.

"Then fucking do something already," Leander said as he unbuckled his belt and pulled out his rigid cock. Underneath me, I could feel Janus's twin cock hard and poking my belly. Oh God, I had missed this. All three of them, focused in on me and our mutual pleasure. Nothing else in the whole world except us.

And then Janus's hand was suddenly on my pussy. Except... it didn't quite feel like a hand. I frowned a little. I tried to look down underneath my body, but Janus's cock bulging in his pants blocked my sight.

"Milo," Janus barked, "paint her lips with precum. Now."

And then the pressure at my pussy started to *buzz*—and *oh*! Oh! It started to suction. Like a mouth but more intense. And the *buzzing*.

"How long do you think?" Leander asked.

I squirmed, almost falling on Janus, the pleasure hitting was so intense, so pleasurable—

"Oh! Oh, oh!"

"You kidding? With as primed as she is? Most women come in a minute with this damn thing. She'll be gone in twenty seconds."

"OOOOOOOOOOOOOOOOoooh!" I screamed, digging my nails into the couch right as Milo started rubbing the tip of his cock over the lips of my open mouth.

"There it is," Janus said, rearing back and smacking my ass again.

Then I heard a slurping sound before Leander's hands were roughly jerking my ass cheeks apart. "Oh fuck, I've missed you."

A sweet sentiment, except I wasn't sure if he was talking to me or my ass. I was pretty sure it was to my ass.

Because the next thing I felt was his thick, fat cock pressing in at my tiny rosebud anus that had shrunk back down to size in the last month and a half since I'd last been breached there.

"Oh *Gooooooooooood*," I groaned, my voice dropping an octave as Leander took me in the deep, dark place.

Janus had let up whatever magical device he had against my clit but now he'd pressed it back against me.

"Oh...oh God...oh." How did they make it so good and so intense all at the same time. I was sure that the pressure at my ass was too much and at the same time I also wanted to press back against him.

"Look at you take that big dick so good," Milo said from above me, grabbing his cock and feeding it into my mouth. "I wanna choke you with my cock while he fucks your ass, honey."

And Janus pressed against my clit—

I fucked against Janus and back against Leander in my ass even though it had me screaming around Milo's shaft in my mouth.

"Aw fuck, baby. Yes. Yes, just like that. When we were in the piazza earlier, all I wanted to do was to tear that pretty dress down, see your tits, and do this. I dream about shoving my cock down your throat. Oh fuck, baby. Seeing you swallow my dick like this, I'm gonna lose it."

"She's creaming all over my hand," Janus said. "She can't get enough of the clit-sucker. It's gonna be our new favorite toy when we wanna torture your clit and make you come so many times you beg us to stop."

"Oh fuck," I gasped.

"Language," Leander said and grabbed my ass and spread me even wider. "Now I'm gonna fuck you so you feel it in the morning."

"Oh shit," I hissed.

"Language!"

And then he fucked me like he meant it. Up the ass. Up. The. Ass.

Till I felt he was meeting Milo fucking my mouth.

My men speared me from all sides, disorienting me, the pleasure still spiraling, all of us receiving and taking and grunting and sweating—

"Fuck!" Leander roared, then thrust one more time and I felt him pulsing inside me.

"Swallow everything Milo has to give you, baby. Cum down her throat, Milo. Now."

"Ugh," Milo cried, undignified and raw as he went stiff and shot off like a rocket at Janus's command.

I swallowed cum and choked and swallowed some more.

"Good girl," Janus said, reaching up and grabbing my jaw in a firm grip as Milo held his cock at my lips, bobbing his head in and out, squeezing the last bits of cum out over my lips. "Such a good, good girl."

I felt like a doll in their hands and I loved it. Loved that

I could go completely loose, and let the pleasure cycle through me, wave after wave.

"Help me get her to the bed," Janus said a moment later. I blinked, feeling hazy from pleasure. They'd taken me to the spacey place I loved, where only extreme sex took me.

I stumbled, all of them surrounding me, to the bedroom and the king-sized bed. Janus laid me down in the middle and helped position me. And then he climbed up between my legs and slid right into my wet pussy like he was always meant to be there.

I hadn't even noticed him lose his pants; he was so damn suave. He was a stunt man now, I guessed, and that had to be second only to a magician.

He looked over his shoulder. "Each of you, take a foot. Give her the foot massage of her life."

And then he turned back, all his focus on me. While his thick shaft was rooted so deep inside my core.

Janus's elbows framed each side of my head, and it was like he'd closed out the rest of the world. Hands grasped each of my feet—one touch gentle, the other firm. But when Janus pushed the hair out of my face and tucked it behind my ear, he was the only one I could focus on.

"Hey baby," he said deep.

I blinked up at him, flat on my back and breathing hard. They always took my breath away.

"Hi," I whispered back, and then giggled. But my giggle turned into a groan when he pulled out and then thrust back in.

"It's happening." Janus frowned.

"What?" I lifted my arms to wrap around his neck.

"He's taking me away from you."

His eyes were dark gray in the dim light of the room.

I shook my head and frowned.

Janus leaned down, his groin grinding against mine. "I barely see you anymore." His hand slid down between us. "You're growing my baby."

I clenched around his shaft inside me. "I'm here." I clenched my arms around his neck. "I'm always here for you."

He nuzzled his face against my neck and whispered, "I hope that's true."

I turned my face into his and we kissed as he pulled out and thrust in again. While the others had fucked me, Janus *made love* to me. He made love to me so sweetly and assured me with his body the things his words had promised.

He loved me.

I clutched him to me with every muscle I had. "I love you," I whispered. "No one will ever take me away from you."

He cried out a low, guttural groan, and flooded me deep inside with his seed.

SEVEN

HOPE

THE NEXT MORNING, Janus woke me up. "How are you feeling, honey?"

I blinked up at him and shifted my legs, smiling when I saw his rumpled hair and the creases on his face from the pillow. And remembering last night. They'd all bathed me after, and I still couldn't decide which I loved best—the lovemaking, or the sweet caretaking after.

I paused and assessed my tummy. For the second day in a row, I didn't feel like running for the toilet.

"I'm good," I said, shocked when I meant it.

"Then come to work with us today," he said. "We're actually going into Venice to train on the gondolas. It'll be a beautiful day on the canals. With all the comforts, I promise."

I bit my lip. It *would* be nice to get out of the apartment for more than just a short walk. But a whole day out...

"And Milo can always bring you back to the hotel if it's too much."

I threw my arms around his neck. "Yes!"

I'D ALWAYS HEARD of Venice but had never realized that it was actually a city *off* the coast of Italy. The way the boat driver explained it, it was composed of 117 small islands connected by bridges and canals.

Humanity was officially insane to build a city like this. It made no sense! But the closer the boat got, skipping across the waves, the more the beautiful historic city came into view. All along the outer edges, docks were surrounded by floating gondolas and boats.

My stomach had even survived the slapping waves of the sea. Thank goodness it was a calm day and the waves hadn't been too strong. Still, when we switched from the wave-runner to a gondola to head deeper into the city, I was glad. The waters were much calmer.

About an hour later, the guys had me perched on a comfortable canvas chair in a sun-dappled mini-courtyard, watching the twins attempt to learn how to steer a gondola. A scene in the movie required Leander's character to steal one and suavely navigate it through the streets of Venice, escaping the bad guy. Hence, needing to look semi-convincing at standing and steering the aforementioned longboat.

Janus got the hang of it right away as the instructor led them through the spiel about the proper way to let the oar enter the water. Then he demonstrated exactly when and how to rotate it so that it cut smoothly through and propelled the craft forward. It looked so easy when he showed them.

But when Leander tried, he tended to dip too deep, so that by the time he got to the pivot and pull part of the rotation, his boat barely moved at all.

"Shallow strokes, shallow strokes!" the instructor called out from right beside me on the dock.

Leander cussed as his gondola started to spin in a circle while Janus's slid smoothly forward.

"No, no, I said shallow strokes!" the instructor called again, then let out a long string of Italian. Milo lifted his eyebrows, looking up from his phone for a second before glancing back down.

I hid a smile. It was so rare to see Leander not immediately excel at anything he tried. He looked over at his brother, whose gondola was twenty feet ahead of him down the canal. Then Leander's brow scrunched in concentration and he swung the oar into the water again. And he *dug* it in, the exact opposite of what the instructor had been asking him to do.

Instead of simply spinning the gondola, though, this time the oar went in deep and got stuck. But Leander still had such a tight grip on the oar, when it caught, his momentum kept moving.

I shoved my hand out, as if I could catch him—even though he was so far away, but he lost his footing and his body pitched forward.

"Leander!" I screeched, but too late. One second Leander was wobbling on the gondola, and the next second his arms were wheeling comically.

Then there was a *splash*.

And Leander disappeared under the water.

EIGHT

HOPE

"LEANDER," I screamed again, jumping up off the comfortable canvas chair Milo and Janus had arranged for me.

From up ahead, Janus swung around and looked back, hand over his eyes to see what was happening. "Leander!" he shouted, then looked ready to jump in after his brother.

But right then Leander's head popped up. He spat out water and splashed his arms.

"Don't swallow!" called the stunt assistant from right beside me, running right up to the edge of the canal while the gondola instructor flattened himself on the ground and held out an oar towards Leander. "For Christ's sake, don't swallow."

I jumped and looked at the stunt assistant. "What happens if he swallows?!"

Leander kept spitting out water while he swam through the mucky canal towards us at the edge.

"Fuck," the stunt assistant said, pulling out his phone. "Katherine Hepburn fell in when they were shooting *Summertime* and she was sick the rest of production!"

"Then why didn't you give them lifejackets!" I cried.

"No one ever falls in," the gondola instructor said helpfully while he thrust the oar a little further out. Leander grasped hold of it and the instructor hauled him in.

Janus rowed himself back to us and smoothly leapt back to the dock right in time to lean down and help pull his brother onto dry land.

Leander glared at him and pulled his arm away from both him and the gondola instructor as he pulled himself up onto the cobbled stone.

"Shit, shit, shit." Brian paced up and down, thumbs flying on the phone.

"Not fucking helpful, Brian," Leander said as he flopped onto his back, heaving for breath.

I hurried to him, alongside Janus, Milo, and the stunt assistant, who I assumed to be Brian.

"No, you don't understand," Brian said. "Hepburn got *really* sick. Is your tetanus shot up to date? Fuck, Kenji's gonna have my ass for this. He told me not to fuck anything up on his day off and I—"

"Shut up, Brian," Leander and Janus said at the same time.

"I have to get him to the hospital," Brian said to Janus, and I could see by Leander's face that he was pissed off at being talked over.

"I don't need to go to—"

Brian's attention switched to Leander quick enough at that. "Oh no, you *have* to get checked out. It's in your contract. You're only allowed to do some of your own stunts if upon any incident you immediately seek medical care. It's a contingency of your insurance."

"Jesus Christ," Leander said, ignoring Janus's arm to help him up, getting to his feet and slinging some canal sludge from his sleeve as he went. "Fine. I'll go."

Janus started to move in the same direction when Brian went on alert. "Whoa, where are you going?"

Janus glared at him. "With my brother."

Brian shook his head vigorously. "This is the whole point of you. You know how tight our schedule is. We have twelve hours blocked out for gondola training and that's *it*." Brian looked down at his phone and swore. "Shit, that's the producer. Look man, just get your ass back on that gondola and don't give us any more trouble than your fuck-up brother."

I watched Janus's jaw harden.

Then he reached out, snatched the phone out of Brian's hand, and threw it in the canal.

"Wha—?" Brian's voice suddenly rose an octave in disbelief. The gondola instructor behind him laughed and I had to say, Brian's face was pretty damn priceless. I don't mind bullies getting some of their own medicine. "You can't do that! I'm your— Your—"

"You're certainly not my fucking boss," Janus said, but Leander swung back around towards us. He looked saggy and water-logged.

"Stay and learn how to do it fucking right," Leander

called. "We both know it'll be you on the damn celluloid for this one."

Then Leander turned and headed around the corner. I wasn't even sure where he was headed. Maybe into the bathroom to get dry? Should I go in and check on him?

But Milo cut me off, "You stay here. I'll go with him."

"Should I—" I started but Milo shook his head.

"He's too proud. Leave him alone for a bit and let him walk it off. I'll make sure he gets to the doctor to be checked out."

I nodded and reached out to squeeze his hand.

"Text updates, yeah?" Janus said. Milo nodded, then he jogged off after Leander.

"How are you feeling?" Janus turned to me. Behind him, Brian was on hands and knees at the edge of the water peering into the canal like he might catch a glimpse of his phone.

"Me?" I asked, surprised. "I'm fine. Why?"

He nodded down at my stomach. "I just thought all the excitement might have—"

I crossed my arms over my chest. "I *know* you are not insinuating that I'm some fainting lily. Women have been birthing babies since the beginning of time and then getting right back into the fields."

Janus stepped into my space and bent down so that his face was an inch from mine. "No woman of mine works in a field."

I pretended to be offended. "That's classist and—"

Janus pulled me to his chest and kissed me.

And kissed me and kissed me. I melted into his hardness. And forgot where we were. I forgot everything except the feel of Janus claiming me.

When he finally pulled back, thankfully still holding me in the frame of his arms because I wasn't sure how steady my jelly legs would be at the moment, he called to Brian and anyone else who might care, "I'm taking lunch. Be back in an hour."

Brian looked up at us and swore but the gondola instructor just smiled and nodded.

My cheeks flushed with heated embarrassment, but also pride.

Janus curled an arm around my shoulder and started leading me towards the opposite corner of the courtyard that Leander left from.

It made me feel like a queen every time Janus claimed me as his in public. I knew it wasn't Leander's fault, and as a publicist I understood better than anyone why he couldn't be seen to be romantically involved with me—*especially* after what happened with their last publicist.

But being able to be myself and show my love with Janus no matter where we were or who was watching?

Well, it was nice to not be someone's secret.

"Shouldn't you be hanging around and proving to them why they hired you?" I asked.

Janus just smirked at me. "I'm proving exactly how much we're both worth. And everyone deserves a lunch break."

"You're taking me to lunch?" I arched an eyebrow.

He just smiled. "You worry too much, anyone ever told you that? Life is here for living. Not to spend so much time worrying."

His arm slid off my shoulder as we reached a narrow alley between tall buildings. Above us, damp white table-cloths fluttered on laundry lines slung between buildings. He took my hand instead.

"You're in one of the most romantic cities in the world with one of the most handsome *men* in the world." He winked at me.

I laughed at his arrogance, even if he only spoke the truth. "Where are we going?"

But he just put a finger over his mouth with his other hand. "It's a secret."

He pulled me through a low archway, then around a corner and—

"Oh!" I cried when we came upon another canal. Thankfully, there was a railing but still. This insane city.

"Here we are."

"Where?" I asked, looking around. It looked like a dead end of a canal. Much of Venice that I'd seen so far was scenic and beautiful, but this was a back alley if I'd ever seen one.

"Here," Janus said, his voice deeper. He opened a little gate and stepped down a step and out onto a waiting gondola I hadn't even noticed. It was sitting low on the water. I looked around, scandalized even though no one was there.

"What are you doing? Get off. What if the owner comes back?"

"What was I just saying?" Janus grinned at me impishly. "Live a little. And they won't. I promise." He winked.

I narrowed my eyes at him.

"Do you trust me?" He held a hand out.

Dammit, it was the same question his twin had asked me once, before inviting me to do something similarly reckless and dangerous.

But these boys. They'd put a spell over me. Because I gave in just as eagerly this time as I had then.

How could I not, with that look of boyish excitement on his face?

So I stepped onto the gondola and he immediately gestured for me to sit down.

When I did, I noticed several fluffy quilts laid out that created a lovely cushioning.

Janus sat down opposite me and grabbed the oar. But he didn't push out into the canal and give me my own private gondola ride like I thought he was going to do. Instead, he moved the oars in the water the opposite direction so that we—

...we slid underneath an archway cut into the building overhead.

It was cool and shadowed away from the sun.

"Finally," Janus breathed out. He was serious now as he sat forward and put a hand on my face. "I've been waiting forever to get you alone."

NINE

HOPE

"NOW THAT YOU have me alone, what will you do with me?" I giggled, still looking around to make sure no one could see us. It was private on the gondola, hidden underneath the archway of the building above us. And yet still public, because anyone could pass by the canal and see.

"This," Janus said, and leaned down to kiss me, pressing me into the quilts that had been laid out on the gondola.

I tilted backwards under his body weight and my arms flew around his neck.

"Janus!" I squealed.

"God, I love hearing my name on your lips," he breathed out, kissing up my neck. "Say it again."

"Janus," I said, shivering under the way his kisses felt.

His hands started to move over my body and I laughed and put my hand on his. "Wait."

He immediately stopped and sounded alarmed, "What? Is it the baby?"

"No, no." I took his hands in mine. "It's just, like you said. We're finally alone. And we never get time to talk. It's one of the nice things about having so much time with Milo. I'm really getting to know him. But I haven't had that time with you. It's all been so"—I shook my head—"such a whirlwind."

He tilted his head and cracked a smile at me, running a hand up my leg. "You know me better than anyone else, honey."

I lifted a hand and caressed it down his face. "I wish that were true. It feels insane to love someone that I barely know anything about."

His brow scrunched. "What do you mean? You know all the important things. How I spend my days. What I eat." He leaned in, pressing his body against mine. "My preferences for how I like to spend my nights."

I rolled my eyes.

"But I don't know what makes you tick. You're so excited for the baby but you haven't even told me why. I had to learn from Milo that you've always wanted a family."

His eyes clouded over a little. "Milo told you that?"

"He really cares about you guys."

Janus made a disgruntled noise. "Maybe he should mind his own business."

"Maybe he wouldn't have to get involved if you and Leander would just talk *to* me sometimes."

Janus sighed and nodded. He pulled back from me to sit on the bench opposite me, but still kept a hand on my knee.

"Okay. What do you wanna know? I'm up for a round of twenty questions."

"Really?" I perked up.

"You're too excited by this." He shook his head, looking amused.

"No, I'm just curious."

"Well, I do like my kitten curious. So ask away."

"Why'd you quit acting? Do you miss it?"

He coughed out a laugh. "Wow, you aren't throwing any punches. And that was two questions. I tell you what. You get one question for every one I ask you. And you don't get to ask them all at once. Let's say...you get one for every orgasm."

I brightened. "Every one of my orgasms? Then I'll have all the questions I want."

"Oh, come on, we have to make it a challenge." He smirked. "Every one of *my* orgasms."

I arched an eyebrow. "Then I better get to work." I dropped down onto my knees in the bottom of the boat and reached for his belt buckle. "Because I have ever so many questions."

"Oh fuck, baby," he hissed out as I reached inside his soft, worn jeans.

"That's the idea," I whispered as I pulled out his heavy cock. He was already hard and getting even firmer in my hand. I smiled, then blew over the tip of his already glistening cock head. Above me, I felt his body tremor where he sat on the little bench. It was quite satisfying to see the effect I had on him.

But I wasn't trying to draw this out today. I wanted

quick and dirty. I wanted to get him off fast. To show myself and him that I could drive him crazy. Beyond his control.

So I took him in my mouth and as far down my throat as I could. Then I gripped him with my mouth, clamping down hard. I pulled back with my head, lips still suckered tight around him. My mouthed made a slick *pop* noise when I came off him all the way, like I was sucking a lollipop.

Above me, he swore. Then his hands dropped down and tangled in my hair. "Goddamn, baby. That's so fucking good," he groaned.

I continued that for several more minutes, winding him up higher and higher till he was fucking my face.

That was when I let my teeth out to scrape slightly down his shaft when he next pulled out. I also reached up to grab his ball-sack hard, digging my fingernails in.

His next thrust in he swore loudly and came like a fire-hose down my throat. I hummed in satisfaction and swallowed all he had to give me.

When I pulled back, I smiled up at him like the cat that got the cream. And really, wasn't that what I was exactly? I certainly felt like curling up in his lap and purring myself to sleep. God, he was beautiful in this light. In every light.

He looked down at me, and his eyes were shining with spent pleasure. "You're so fuckin' perfect."

Then he slid down beside me. There was still quilting down here—it had been spread out over the entire gondola —but it was a tight fit with the both of us. Janus didn't seem to mind; he just wrapped his arms around me and drew me close.

"You want to know why I always wanted a family?" he asked, breath wafting my air in the cool afternoon shadows.

I nodded against his chest.

"Because I always wanted *this*. A woman who gives me a blow job 'cause she loves me. Snuggling with her afterwards. My kid in her belly. Knowing she'll always be there for me and I'll do the same for her. Having a family means having a center in this world, a home to always come back to. And hell yeah, I always wanted that for myself. Leander and me were on our own from such a young age. Even after Milo's mom adopted us. Maybe especially then."

"Do you remember your mother? Your bio mom, I mean?"

Janus shrugged, then arched an eyebrow at me. "That's another question."

"Oh, come on—"

"Kidding, I'm kidding." He narrowed his eyes at me. "Mostly. But I'll give this one as a freebie since you just sucked all my brains out through my dick." He sat back against the bench of the gondola. "Do I remember Mom? Hmm." He looked down, into the murky canal water. "We were so young when she and Dad were taken away."

His eyes seemed to gloss over a little, but he still answered. "But yeah, I remember a little about her. I don't remember my dad at all, but I remember Mom always smelled good. It was a good life—I just remember I was always happy before we went to live with—"

His face went dark suddenly, and it was like I could feel him close off.

"Anyway, we better get back." He caressed a hand through my hair. "I don't know how far I can push Brian. Kenji told me to take it easy with him since it's his first day."

"He's not even doing anything," I protested. "Just standing around."

"Yeah, but him being here means Kenji can have a day off, and Kenji I respect."

I hated giving up this time with him but nodded. He *was* here to work. I'd hoped to connect more than squeezing the tiny little bit of information I had out of him. Would it always be like this? A drip instead of a fountain?

But then, didn't actions speak louder than words? And when it came to actions, Janus had always been the first to demonstrate he cared.

"If I have to let you go, I will," I said mournfully, still getting up to pull myself off of him.

Then he grabbed hold of me and looked down between us. So I did too.

And there was his cock, again jutting red-veined and angry back up at us. I frowned, confused, because I definitely knew he'd come already. Good Lord, the evidence was still coating the lining of my throat.

"Well fuck, they can wait a little longer," Janus said. "It hasn't quite been an hour yet,"

The responsible part of me wanted to say no, no, we should go back to training like good, grownup adults.

The rest of me was gleeful when Janus shoved in between my legs and started pushing into my wetness with his cock still wet from my saliva. I'd get another question, I reasoned. I could learn more about him.

Or I was just a horny slut. Because I groaned low with how good he felt as he maneuvered us sideways on the gondola and really started thrusting into me. The boat rocked with our motions.

Especially when Janus started whispering into my ear, "You're everything I've ever wanted, Hope. You're the woman of my dreams. And I know you're going to be an amazing mother to both this kid and the others I eventually plant in you."

My mouth dropped open. Children? Children, as in *plural?!*

But I didn't have time to sputter or ask questions, because the first waves of pleasure were hitting.

Janus covered my mouth with his and kissed me until I was shuddering and quivering with pleasure.

TEN

HOPE

EVERYTHING CHECKED out fine at the doctor's office with Leander. They gave him an updated tetanus shot and some antibacterial drops for his eyes. Otherwise, he was supposed to watch and wait for any other symptoms. Awesome. If he got sick from the water, they'd give him the full round of antibiotics. If not, then the doctor thought he'd be just fine.

This was news gained second hand from Milo, because Leander was a storm cloud when we got back home later that night.

But it turned out, that was only the beginning.

Not that I knew it then. It seemed like things were finally getting on track. No, I didn't find time to talk to Janus more about all the questions I wanted to ask him—and believe me, I was keeping track of every orgasm he had and storing up my questions! It was just a matter of finding time with him alone. It seemed he was always on the run between the stunt training and workouts.

On the bright side, my nausea continued calming down. I'd heard that could happen in the second trimester. After feeling like death-warmed-over all first trimester, though, I hadn't dared hope. But apparently, I had turned the corner... and suddenly I could eat again.

And I wanted to eat *everything*. Meat. Cheese. Pastries. It was like that one slice of pizza in the piazza that day had opened up a monster inside me. An ever hungry, never satisfied monster.

The doctor told me to keep an eye on it when I'd let them know I'd actually *lost* weight in the first month of pregnancy. Well, they were gonna be delighted on my next visit, because I was definitely making up for it now.

Better late than never, Janus kept remarking, while smacking my ever-more-voluptuous ass. And I'd had plenty to begin with.

I'm glad at least *they* were appreciating the changes that were beginning to be noticeable in my body. I just kept knocking into things, my new proportions throwing off my balance. Because, yeah, I was suddenly... uh... top-heavy.

My boobs.

I'm talking about my boobs.

They'd gotten noticeably bigger... and well, *bouncier*. Milo liked to lie in bed and just poke them to watch them jiggle. He'd get this big ol' grin on his face like his life-long dreams were finally coming true.

I could only roll my eyes.

My bras barely fit and they were double Ds to begin with. I didn't even know what size comes after that? Triple

D? G? Maybe I'd just abandon bras altogether and start wearing stretchy fabric bands I'd seen online—they weren't especially attractive but looked comfy as hell. And comfy was my new favorite word.

The last two weeks we'd been ordering in—delicious meal after delicious meal—because *Trapdoor*, Leander's latest movie, had premiered here in Italy. It had turned into a global blockbuster, and the Italians were falling just as hard for Leander's rising star.

Hence, we were having a harder time getting around the city than when we first arrived. It wasn't like back in New York *yet*, but the twins were getting recognized more and more.

Tonight, though, tonight they said they had a surprise and Milo promised I didn't need to worry, they'd taken care of everything. We were riding in the car towards a mystery destination. They'd even made me wear a blindfold so I couldn't see where they were taking me—as if I'd have any idea where we were going anyway!

Leander and Janus had finished their training and tomorrow shooting started on the actual movie. I thought they might want to spend their last free night with the cast and crew, but Janus had looked at me like I was crazy.

To my surprise, Leander said he wanted to come with us too.

I wasn't sure exactly why, but ever since the night he'd finally given in and slept with me again, he'd been different. Not quite so in-your-face-assholish.

I wouldn't go so far as to say the tumble in the water had quenched his ego. It would take far more than a dip in some mucky canal water for that. And I doubted he'd changed his tune or his mind about me or the baby. I still saw the distrust in his eyes when he looked at me.

That didn't stop him from rejoining our bed, though. And he didn't pull away from my touch anymore, either. He was just as quick to reach for me as Janus or Milo these days.

So some part of him still wanted me, even if he didn't want to admit it.

I wasn't sure how I felt about that. I didn't want to be wanted against someone's will or better judgement. I deserved better.

But if I wasn't quite sure how to deal with Leander or how I felt about him, things between me and Janus and me and Milo were solidifying. I was growing a firm foundation with them. Something that just might grow into... well, into a *family*.

I glowed at the word, caressing it in my mind. Me, who'd always had such a negative association with the word. But the guys were showing me that family, when it was people you *chose*—could actually feel like a home.

"Okay, keep your eyes shut," Janus said, and I could hear the smile in his voice even though I couldn't see him.

"Why?" I laughed. "You have a blindfold on me. I can't see a thing."

"Good," Milo said. "That's the point. We're trying to surprise you."

"You realize just getting out of the apartment is a great surprise. Now let me see! I want to look around. I never get to go anywhere!"

"I don't know." Janus's voice was heavy with teasing. "Should we let her see where we are?"

Leander's voice was less playful. "Well, the sun's almost down, so if you want her to see anything you better take the damn eye mask off."

"Never any fun, oh brother of mine," Janus muttered, and then I felt the blindfold being lifted off my head.

I blinked against the rays of sunset splashed across the stunning city. The oranges and yellows and creams of the buildings stood out against the cooling, darkening sky. Especially as twinkling lights turned on all throughout the city.

"So where are we?" I asked.

"At the best restaurant in the city," Janus grinned. "Now that you can eat, we thought we'd give you the best to put in your mouth."

"That's what she said," Milo quipped as he popped out from the driver's seat to hurry around to my door. He didn't open it right away, though.

I laughed, always delighted when his dirty mind popped out into the open other than during sexy times. Apparently, his mind was always in the gutter, from the things he related when we were in bed, but usually he gave zero intimation of it.

"Why did I need a blindfold for that?" I asked Janus.

"Because there's a theme to tonight." Then he finished by whispering in my ear: "Anticipation. And giving up control."

I shivered and felt my sex clench up at the single word. And the feel of his warm breath at my ear.

"Now be a good girl and open up. I need you to keep this wet for Daddy." He pulled something out of his inner jacket pocket and then was pressing cool glass against my lips.

I opened my mouth, barely able to look down and see the glass balls on a thick black thread before Janus was popping them in my mouth. They clicked against my teeth.

"That's a good girl." His voice was low and gritty. My sex clenched again. I could feel myself swelling. *God*, what these men did to me. It was unseemly.

"Now *suck*," Janus said, lingering on the last syllable.

I suckled the balls in my mouth, my eyes locked on Janus's. His glittered in the late afternoon light.

Never breaking eye-contact, he shoved his forefinger and thumb between my lips and plucked one bead out. Then he tugged, slowly pulling the string out bead by bead. My lips plumped and puckered over each round glass bulb as it passed by.

"That's a pretty pet," Janus breathed out.

He pulled the last ball past my lips, then yanked up my skirt with his other hand. He was rough, and it made me wet, knowing we were both giving into our animalistic sides out in the open like this—just a car door away from, well, everyone—

He yanked down my panties and then his thick fingers were parting my puffy, fat folds, plunging in until—

"Oh," I gasped out, reaching forward to clutch the seat back in front of me as the first bulbous round was pressed against my pussy.

Janus rolled it around in my swollen flesh, getting it good and wet as if my saliva hadn't been enough—

"That's right, pretty little slut. Let me feed this in this sweet, sweet cunt."

I clenched around the glass and then released, and Janus didn't miss the moment to shove the ball up my wet—

"Oh dear God—" I squeaked out just as Janus yanked my panties up and my dress down. He put his mouth to my ear again. "No taking these out during dinner. I want you on edge and tortured the entire fucking time, do you hear me, pet? Say yes, Sir."

I gasped in a breath and barely managed an audible, "Yes, Sir," right as Milo grinned and pulled the door open out onto the bright, glittering Italian sunset. "Buona sera, Bella!"

ELEVEN

HOPE

A VALET STEPPED into the front seat and drove the car away. I braced myself on Milo and Janus's arms. My legs were jelly. Leander exited the car out the other side. I could feel his eyes on me and his brother.

I tried to suck in a deep, steadying breath as I adjusted to the feel of the string of glass beads in my—

Look at the view. Yes, that was a lovely distraction. And it truly was a gorgeous view. The restaurant was in sight of the *Prato della Valle*, or *Il Prato* as I'd heard a couple of locals call it.

History. Perfect. La la la, boring history. Deep breath in.

And I mean, it was amazing to see in real life what I'd only read about in the guides online. This town square was ancient. It had an oval canal in the center and there had been chariot races around it and shit like that in Roman times. Then later, *executions*.

I grew up in Nevada and mostly, the only old stuff we had there was dirt.

Now *Il Prato* was a marketplace. People bustled all through the square, buying things or simply out for an evening walk with their kids. Such a different vibe than back home.

Milo tugged on my arm and I knew my moment of centering myself and gathering any peace was over. Especially when my pussy tingled with every step as the glass balls slipped and slid around inside me.

Oh yeah, I was jumping back into the whirlwind with them headfirst. My spine tingled in anticipation...along with, well, other places. I was ready. I'd been shut up in that damn apartment for too long.

More than ready. Especially after the disaster last time we'd all gone out together. I was young, I was out with gorgeous men, and it was officially time to make and stack up some *good* memories. We'd come a long way, baby. Well —I bit my lip as I let myself be led inside the Michelin star restaurant by the guys—thinking of the *actual baby* inside me, I certainly hoped we had.

"Watch out," Leander said from in front of me, turning back and grasping me by my arm and around my back at my waist. "There's a step here. Be careful."

I blinked, hypersensitive from how Janus had been touching me and—

I glanced up at Leander. I wasn't sure what I read in his gray-silver eyes. But we paused there a moment. I thought I detected a slight frown on his forehead. Because we were touching? Was he feeling the same electricity?

I nodded. "I-I-I'll be careful." Then I ducked my head,

stepping forward, embarrassed by my stutter. I hated that it showed my emotions like that.

Had to admit, though. This was certainly a different Leander than the one who'd been chaining me to a bed a month and a half. So maybe we really had made progress?

"Hope."

I stopped, turning around. Leander stood there in the foyer of the restaurant, the walls a burnished Tuscan gold. There was a halo of light behind his hair. It was as if the man always took studio lighting around with him wherever he went. So damn annoying.

But the earnest look on his face had my heart softening and opening to whatever he was about to say—

Which was naturally interrupted when a woman suddenly came banging in the door of the restaurant. She was older but fit, with badly dyed blonde hair and clothing that my best friend Mikayla would have described as... tacky, to be polite.

"Signora, you must have a reservation!" The hostess tried to step in front of her but she wasn't having it.

The woman just fluttered her manicured hand in the air like a butterfly and pranced right past the stunned hostess, heading straight for Leander.

"Leander. Honey. How hard is it to pick up the phone and call your *mother*?"

Mother?!?!

I couldn't help the squeak that came out of my throat as I clenched around the balls still tucked up inside my cooch.

TWELVE

HOPE

THE HOSTESS LOOKED towards Leander and Janus, confusion on her face. She sputtered out in beautifully accented English, "She is... with you?"

"Yes," Janus said at the same time Leander spat, "*No.*"

Then they both glared at each other.

"We agreed last time," Leander growled.

"But the—" Janus broke off but looked my way.

I could hear what he hadn't said. *The baby.* Their adoptive mother—Milo's bio mom—looked at me, and her face brightened. Janus wanted the baby to know their grandmother. My heart squeezed. Along with the muscles in my sex. Dear God, what if I somehow lost grip on the glass balls and they slipped out? I was embarrassingly wet at the moment. I clenched all my muscles.

"Is it right for a mother to hear about her son's *engagement* from the tabloids instead of a phone call?" She shook a finger at Janus and then smiled at me, bleached white teeth gleaming even in the dim foyer lighting. "And you must be Hope, the woman who finally got one of my boys to grow up and *commit*."

Her attention ping-ponged back to Leander. "Although maybe wedding bells will be catching? Everywhere I go online all I read about is *Lender* this and *Lender* that." Then she looked around. "Is Lena here with you now? I heard she was vacationing nearby so the two of you could canoodle while you worked on the new movie."

"Jesus fucking Christ," Leander swore, pulling away from her and yanking out his phone. "Hope," he barked.

I already had my phone out too. "I'm on it." We'd been monitoring the Lena rumors and trying to control the narrative, mostly successfully. Our spin: yes, Leander and Lena liked to flirt for the cameras but that was all just in good fun. *Really,* they were only close friends, not romantically involved anymore.

But I hadn't heard Lena was vacationing in Italy. Just because we were trying to control the narrative didn't mean Lena liked it. I didn't put it past her to try to stir shit up if she was anywhere in a hundred-mile radius.

I'd barely started hunting any info down when their mother said, "Well, what are we all doing here standing around? Aren't we going to eat dinner? I've come all this way."

"We have a reservation," Leander said coldly. "You don't."

"Leander," Janus said, grabbing his brother's arm. "Don't you think family might be more important now than ever?"

"I think what's important is to remember that people don't change. Milo, back me up here."

I looked over to where Milo stood in the corner of the lobby, silent, watching the exchange between his mother and adoptive brothers. She hadn't said a single word to him yet.

Only now, once Leander brought attention to him did she turn to her other son.

"Milo, honey." She flashed her bright beauty-pageant grin. She was a beautiful woman, or you could tell she once had been. She looked worn now, her skin tight in places where she'd obviously had work done—not very skilled work—and sagging in others.

Leathery-tan, extra-large fake breasts were hiked up in a gravity-defying bra, showcased by a blouse that bared an incredible amount of cleavage for a woman of any age. I averted my eyes so I didn't accidentally catch a nip slip.

"Milo, honey," she repeated as she approached Milo. "I've missed you so much. I'd love to catch up. Pretty please." Her voice was high-pitched and she made praying hands.

To be honest, she was starting to make a bit of a scene. I saw Milo's eyes darting around and maybe that was what he was thinking as he nodded grimly. He put an arm around her shoulders and guided their mom deeper into the restaurant.

Leander threw his arms out like, *what the hell?* But Janus just put a hand at the small of my back and I went forward, eyebrows raised. Well, this had taken a turn. Especially when I couldn't help the little squeak that came out at the quick steps to keep up with Janus's long strides. When he looked down at me with a grin, I knew *he* knew exactly what had elicited it. These damn glass balls!

Unlike his brothers, Janus seemed perfectly fine with their trainwreck of a mother showing up out of the blue. But I hadn't forgotten all that Milo had told me about her. I wasn't inclined to give her the benefit of the doubt. I'd known too many stage mothers like her in the business. Obsessed with living through their children's celebrity...

But there wasn't any time to ask Janus anything about it, because the next second we were in the intimate dining room of the little Italian restaurant. The hostess was quickly arranging for another chair and table setting to be brought to the table that had been set for four.

Leander stalked forward and yanked out a seat to sit in, a storm cloud over his head. The hostess just glanced between us all quickly before hurrying away again, obviously sensing the vibe. Milo sat beside Leander, and it was odd to see him so tightly wound. Usually he was the easy, fun one when the rest of us were tense.

Their mother turned to Janus and started chatting at him. I could only say *at* him because it didn't seem required that he respond. Or that anyone was listening. She just seemed like one of those people who never stopped talking.

"I had such a *time of it* getting here. You would not believe the delays I had to endure! At Heathrow we were on the tarmac for forty-five minutes. Forty-five minutes, can you believe that! And I was in coach. Coach. Can you even *see* me riding in coach?"

She shook her head in disgust. "I mean, during the *Who's Counting Now* years, we all rode in the best of the best. Private jets. Or at least *first class*. Oh," she laughed, putting a hand on Janus's arm as she sat down in the center chair of the three left empty. Which effectively forced Janus to seat me beside Milo and then take the seat beside Leander, several chairs away from me.

I didn't know whether to be a little offended or touched that Janus wouldn't ask his mother to move so he could sit by me.

I was his...fiancée? Or was I?

There had never been a ring and we hadn't discussed it outside of his spontaneous proposal that night a month ago. Not with him working so much. I mean, how exactly was it supposed to work if we got married? Would we still... be a group along with Milo and Leander? Or was asking to marry me trying to lay some kind of singular claim on me. Was that what I wanted?

I reached for the glass in front of me when I saw Janus taking his mom's hand.

And as if reading my mind: "Mama, will you switch seats with me? I hate to abandon my fiancée to Milo over there. He's too charming."

She'd been in the middle of a stream of saying something, but she glanced over at me again, as if only now remembering my presence since first acknowledging me. "Oh! I guess that makes sense."

But she didn't react at all to the word *fiancée*. At least not when it came to Janus. I could only stare at her. She'd made such a big deal of *rumors* about Leander and Lena, but now here her other son was telling her that he *was* getting married and she was barely—

She grabbed the table and the back of her chair. "God,

my back just aches so much to get up and down like this," she winced.

"No," I said, hurriedly at the exaggerated look of pain on her face. "It's fine. I don't mind the seating arrangements."

"Oh, honey," she said, putting a hand on my arm now. "You're such a dear to an old woman. Now do tell me. How did you snare my little boy? They've dated *models*." She squinted at me, obviously not seeing anything in me as worthy as a *model*.

I laughed low. *Wow, lady*, I thought, but didn't say it. I just tilted my head and smiled the smile my momma did in church when she said, *well, bless your heart*.

"I guess I charmed them."

Her smile dropped and her eyes narrowed like she was sniffing out a clue. "Them?"

Shit. Maybe she was smarter than I'd given her credit for. And probably more dangerous. I fought to keep the saccharine smile on my face. "Yes, I charmed both of them to get the job. It's called an interview."

"Or did you come work for them because of those nasty rumors?" she asked, eyes narrowed. "*Trying* to charm one or both of my boys and get them wrapped around your finger? Janus is a sweetheart. He'll fall for anything."

"Mom!" Janus said at the same time Leander rolled his eyes. "Here we go."

"She's not wrong," Milo whispered vehemently, sitting forward. "He is too gullible, because he keeps falling for your shit." He glared at their mom. "Why are you really here, Mom? Do you need money? Just tell us how much.

Enough with this dog and pony show like you actually care."

Her mouth dropped open. "I *do* care. If any of you would actually *answer* my calls or texts—"

"You mean the ones you leaked last time Janus texted?" Leander said scathingly.

"I told you, my phone was hacked!" she exclaimed. "Janus, honey, you believe me, don't you? I'd never do anything to hurt you. I miss my boys. I hate missing out on your lives. Please. You're getting married and I just want—"

But a growing noise made all of us look towards the foyer. The hostess had her hands out, but there was a crowd pushing past her. Many of whom had cameras and phones up.

A waiter had run over to join the hostess but they were barely holding people back who had started shouting:

"Leander!"

"Can I get a picture?"

"Leander! I love you! Will you marry me?"

"Leander!"

And then it just turned into a roar.

"Jesus, what did you do?" Leander asked, throwing the napkin he'd only just spread on his lap on the table as he shoved his chair back and jumped up. Immediately he and Janus were by my side.

"They must've followed me," their mom said. "The paparazzi track my every step."

"Because you call them," Milo growled, stepping in front of me to block me from view of the cameras. "Get her out of here."

"Let's all get out of here," Janus hissed. "You always have a backup plan. What's the secondary exit?"

"Alley out back," Milo said. "Hurry."

Janus grabbed my hand, turning quickly to his mom. And his face—whoa. I'd never seen an expression that dark on his features. "This is the last time you disappoint me."

"Honey," their mother called. "Honey, I just thought it would be a great photo op. My social media has really been blowing up lately when I show old videos I took backstage from *Who's Counting Now*. And a shot of us all reuniting with you introducing me to your fiancée—it would just make all our collective fans go so wild! Honey, just listen—"

"Keep her away from me," Janus said to Leander. But Leander was taking my other side. "You deal with her. I told you years ago to cut the bitch off. I have more important matters to see to."

And Leander grabbed my other hand, taking the lead behind Milo as we pushed through swinging doors into the kitchen. It was loud with a different kind of noise, pots and steam and voices shouting orders. White-frocked people scurrying around started yelling at us in Italian.

Milo held up a hand as he kept barging forwards. "*Scusi! Scusi!*"

I was stretched between Leander dragging me forward from the front and Janus trailing from behind, occasionally looking back in the direction of his mother. As if he knew he was saying goodbye to her for the last time.

Finally we were through to the back of the restaurant and Milo shoved the door open roughly with both hands. He exploded out into a dark alley. The rest of us tumbled after.

It was quiet. Until Milo doubled over and absolutely screamed his guts out into his knees. And then, far down the long twisting alleyway, we heard voices and saw phones lighting up the darkness as they snapped pictures.

Some of Leander's fans had obviously figured out we might try to duck out the back. But the restaurant was part of a long block of connected buildings here, like so many were, and the fans had a ways to trek to actually get to us.

So Leander and Janus both started yanking me in the opposite direction at the same time. Again pulling me apart.

"Hey," I gasped. "Wait for me." Or at least wait for me to get my feet underneath me.

They paused, but only to steady me, and then we were rushing forwards again. About fifteen feet ahead of us, another back door opened and a man stepped out with a cigarette to his lips.

"In there," Milo said from behind us.

Leander nodded and let go of my hand to sprint ahead. He grabbed the door to stop it from shutting and held it open for me.

I jumped up the one step to get inside and the boys quickly followed. Janus locked it after us.

"But what about the guy that opened it?" I asked.

"Sorry, he can take the long way round," Leander said. "Your safety is more important."

"Exactly," Janus agreed.

"But—"

I was over-ridden as the men hustled me forwards into... a *club*?

We went down a long black hallway and then came out onto a dance floor that was dark except for flashing lights. It was a Friday night, late because of the twins' schedule. But apparently, even in usually sleepy Padua there was an underground party scene.

"Stay here," Milo said—or rather leaned in and yelled at us to be heard over the music. "I'll go check if it's clear out front. If it is, I'll call and have the car brought from the valet down the street. If not, we might have to call in another ride."

Leander and Janus nodded identically. I fought to hide a smile, even in these crazy conditions. Even with these goddamned glass balls still up my hoo-ha.

The twins were so protective. And to see each of their reactions to their mother, such vulnerabilities, even if they'd played out so oppositely. Leander so hardened, Janus so hopeful, only to have expectations crushed —

Janus grabbed me by my waist and swung me onto the dance floor. I gasped and held onto his shoulders for dear life as I got my feet underneath me. But he was smooth and I never once stumbled.

"What are you doing?" I asked, just a little short of a shriek. Still, I was barely audible above the thumping bass and blaring beat.

He bent over as he slid an arm tighter around my waist. "Blending in."

I felt a heat at my back and glanced over my shoulder. It was Leander. He was facing away from me, but his ass was warm against mine. He was dancing—and not bad for a white guy. But then, Greek men had a special dispensation, I supposed. I was certainly melting into Janus's arms as he pulled me sensually against him.

Janus leaned in again. "You should get lost, bro," he said

over my shoulder. "We tend to attract attention when we're together."

Leander turned his head and yelled through his teeth, "We will if you keep talking to me. Now shut up and do something with those fucking beads."

Was he freaking kidding?! I was about to turn around and tell him ha ha, very funny, when I felt Janus's hand in the darkness of the club, reaching underneath my miniskirt.

Oh, he wouldn't dare.

Leander reached back behind him and grabbed my ass hard at the same time I felt Janus's thick fingers tugging at the end of the string that barely hung out of my pussy. It reminded me of a tampon string. Except tampons didn't make me feel like—

Ohhhhhhh—

I think I groaned as blood rushed my face and pleasure raced all around my sex. I bent my head down onto Janus's chest as a slower, dub-step song came on. He palmed my wet pussy as the bass thundered underneath our feet.

I could not *believe* they were choosing this freaking moment to play. When they *knew* we were in danger of fans mobbing us, when any second—

"*Ahhhhhhhh!*" I squeaked subsonically into Janus's chest, grasping his shirt in my fist. Janus was pulling the string. And each of the glass balls would glide, and then *thud*, glide, and thud, each one tugging on my pussy from the *inside* as it came, hitting *so* many spots at once. It was unholy and downright fucking wicked of them to be doing this to me in public. I couldn't make another noise. I couldn't.

Janus tugged another ball, and this one was the

biggest, I knew it. I remembered the feel of it in my mouth. It had barely passed my teeth. And now Janus was tugging it out of my slick, wet pussy. Tugging and tugging it, and oh god, I felt it on every single surface of every bit of my walls.

Until finally, it *popped* free and I lurched forward into Janus's arms.

But he was ready for me and kept me steady on my feet.

Leander squeezed my ass hard from behind again and then Janus pulled the last three smaller bulbs free.

I gasped as the peaking pleasure made my vision blur, fingernails digging in as my hands fisted his shirt tighter.

"That's fucking right," Janus said in my ear. "Fucking come for Daddy. Come like my gorgeous little slut. You're fucking beautiful. The most amazing thing I've ever seen in my life. Now come again. Harder. Fucking come, you *sweet little fucking slut*."

I spasmed harder than ever as pleasure spiked up and down my spine and back to my clit that Janus's whole hand was massaging now.

"I've got our ride," Milo's voice was suddenly yelling in our ear.

I jerked back from Janus and would have toppled over if he hadn't kept me steady from where he had a solid grip on me—at my pussy. I was still coming. Not fair, not fair. There were serious things— I had to, oh god, oh *god*—

"Goddamn, what are you two doing to her. Fuck. We still have to go. Now. Everyone's gonna start noticing a car with blacked-out windows parked in a no-parking zone three doors down if we don't get our asses out there in the next sixty seconds."

"Fuck," Janus said, pulling his hands away from me. Then he was shoving something towards my face. "Open."

I did on instinct at this point, opening my mouth just in time for it to be shoved full of the glass beads again. They were coated with my own juices this time.

When Milo saw, I heard his low, tortured, "Aw fuck, man."

But then it was Leander dragging the both of them forward while I struggled to close my mouth around all the balls at once. It seemed impossible and yet if I really struggled, I could just barely close my lips over them. I probably looked ridiculous, but maybe that was part of it. Maybe being out of control, and God, I could still feel the pleasure from—

I stopped thinking and just ran, two steps for each of their one, and then we were out the door of the club and back in the night air, several degrees cooler than when we'd entered the restaurant at the start of the evening. Or maybe I was just several degrees hotter at the moment. Dear Lord.

"Here," Milo said, darting forward towards a Fiat. The valet jumped out in time, but instead of Milo jumping behind the wheel, he grabbed Leander's arm, "You," and pointed towards the driver's seat.

Leander didn't argue, likely only because there wasn't time. He jumped in the driver's seat while Janus put me in the back. Milo took shotgun.

And just like that—

The wheels squealed as Leander peeled away.

"Jesus," Janus said. "I don't even have her buckled in yet."

"Well, hurry the fuck up," Leander said, glancing in the

rearview mirror before focusing back on the road. He shifted and pressed the gas, speeding up to hit a green light.

The speed pressed me back against the seat and Milo let out a whoop, then he leaned his seat back.

"Hey man," Janus said, moving to the middle seat to get out of the way.

But then we saw that Milo had... well, intentions. His hands were on his pants buckle. And he was quickly undoing it.

"What?" he asked. "You can't let me walk in on that shit on the club and only give me a glimpse. I need more. I need it— I need—"

He broke off and I saw something in his eyes. And remembered his guttural scream back in the alley way.

So I reached in my mouth, found the end of the string, and plucked the balls out one...by one...by one.

Milo watched in fixated fascination as each one emerged past my lips.

When the last one emerged, I asked, "You need to watch us fuck, Daddy?"

THIRTEEN

HOPE

MILO'S HEAD had ducked slightly but it suddenly lifted all the way up. So had Janus's. The car swerved a little too, when Leander glanced back, but he got hold of it again. Janus smacked him on the back of the head.

"I got it, I got it." Leander sounded resigned. "I drive. You fuck. Crystal clear."

I smiled and turned so that my back was up against the car door. Janus, sitting beside me, reached over and double-checked the door I was leaned against was locked. Which made my heart along with my pussy buzz with warmth.

"Daddy," I whispered, and reached for Janus.

Which he wasn't about to allow.

Janus caught my wrists mid-air and pinned them against the door and the seat. My breath caught. Dear Lord, I loved his dominant side. It made me feel—I couldn't even—just heated and safe and kinky and wrong and right all at the same time—

"I'm going to fuck you now," Janus breathed into my ear.

I nodded. "Please."

I hadn't even seen him pull himself out. But I was wet and ready when I felt his cock at my entrance. I was still throbbing from the club. These men were crazy.

These men were crazy... and I loved them.

So I said it out loud. "I love you."

The spark that lit in Janus's eye—might have just been a passing streetlight—but the way that he leaned down and passionately kissed me. Taking me. Devouring me. Giving me pleasure beyond imagination. That didn't have anything to do with the lighting.

He made love to my mouth, teasing me with his tongue while the head of his cock dipped in and out of my swollen pussy lips.

"Say it again." He reached underneath me, grabbing my ass and shifting me at the same time so he could slide in another inch.

"Oh God," I gasped.

"I have been known to go by that name," Janus said, "now say it again." He thrust forward, burying himself balls deep.

"I love you," I said, straining against his hold at my wrists. I wanted to wrap my arms around his neck.

But he was still letting me know who was in control. Even as he asked for me to give what I could only give freely. My love. Every bit of it drove pleasure higher.

Janus bent over me so far, his teeth were at the base of my neck, nipping me as he said, "Now tell Milo. Tell Milo what we both know is the truth. Let him know, baby, while I fuck you like something out of his best wet dream."

I shuddered, my left leg doing what my arms couldn't—wrapping around his body as he penetrated me. He thrust more furiously than ever. And over his shoulder I looked at Milo in the reclined front seat. He was fisting his cock. Fisting it roughly and jerking himself as he watched Janus fuck me.

"I love you, Milo," I said, heaving for breath, wrists still restrained. "I fucking love you and you know it."

Milo came, long ropey streams shooting out onto the dash. Leander swore but I just licked my lips.

"Oh fuck yeah, Daddy. Do you—"

Janus thrust so hard I was momentarily out of breath.

"—have any more for me?" I finished on a gasp.

Milo made a strained noise and his face contorted. More cum spurted as he jacked himself even harder, eyes never straying from me, from Janus fucking me, from—

I screamed out my orgasm. It was the first time I didn't have to be quiet. Leander had gotten us onto a highway.

So I *howled* as Janus fucked an orgasm out of me and Milo kept fucking his hand long after any cum could possibly be left his balls as he watched Janus continue to fuck the shit out of me.

"I'm about to get off the goddamned highway," Leander growled from the front seat.

Janus grunted above me and thrust, his ass moving up and down as he jerked forward, in and out and in, out, then in again.

He only pulled out when Leander hit an exit ramp.

And then Janus yanked his cock out of me only to grab me and tug me down the back seat so that I was underneath him.

"I'm gonna ruin your pretty dress, little girl." He rubbed his cock over my mouth as I nodded.

"Look at how fucking perfect you are. The only thing that could make you prettier..."

I opened my mouth. He rubbed his cock around my lips. Jesus, I loved this move. I don't know why it made me feel so sensual but it did. Especially when I looked up at his face, where he was watching the tableau of us, transfixed.

It was these moments—these raw bits where I saw them, and felt them inside me, all of us together and naked in every way, being penetrated, and stimulated—that made all the rest of it worth it.

Them giving me pleasure after pleasure, me knowing I was giving them all pleasure and something more.

These weren't the kind of men who went to a therapist when they had feelings about their mother coming into town. They were the kind of men who needed to fuck it out. Different strokes for different folks. Speaking of different strokes...

Janus was stroking his glorious shaft right above me, worshipfully, as the car began to slow.

"There's no more time," Leander said from the front.

And Janus erupted in a stream, coating my dress from top to bottom.

"Jesus, that's the hottest fucking thing I've ever seen," Milo swore, collapsing back on the seat with a smile on his face, hand still stroking his semi.

And then he looked back at me, smile softening—hand never leaving his cock, which made me giggle, as he said—"I love you too, baby."

FOURTEEN

HOPE

MILO WAS as good as his word. He had indeed ruined my dress. Not that any of them seemed to mind in their hurry to get me upstairs. Milo wasn't the only one who had been... Well, willing to channel his emotions into... a more physical approach.

Janus was behind me pushing in the door as soon as Milo had it open. Leander came in right after him.

Janus had my shirt off over my head seconds later and then hands were on my leggings. Leander's hands. For once, the two of them were working in concert together. No words were spoken between them. Between anybody. No. This wasn't about words. This was about a different kind of connection.

Janus reached my hips and yanked me to him, my bare ass against the cool denim of his jeans. His hardness was like a stone against my ass.

"Put her down there," Leander demanded.

But Janus didn't take me to the couch. Instead, he dragged me by my hips over to the kitchen table. Then he flipped me around and pushed me down. Not too hard—I think he was still keeping my pregnancy in mind because even though I could tell he was in a mood, he didn't shove me down or anything. But he was still harsh when he grasped the back of my hair.

"She's going to take our cocks. One after another. She's gonna be our little whore tonight and she's gonna love every fucking second of it. While her daddies run a train on her. Daddy's little whore. Now you better be slick and ready, because this is hard."

He unbuckled his jeans, unbuttoned them and then his cock was— He thrust in my wet pussy.

"Heh God—" I gasped.

He braced one hand on the table so he could fuck me deeper.

"You like that. Your pussy's taking me so good. I think you want it harder."

"Yes. Harder," I managed to gasp out.

"Leander," Janus ordered. "Gag her. She doesn't get to say a word tonight. She's our doll."

Janus spanked my ass and then fucked me even harder.

Leander walked around the table and shoved four fingers in my mouth while his brother fucked me even harder. One hand squeezing my thickening waist, the other clutching the wood of the table so hard his knuckles were white.

Janus's cock was impossibly hard inside me. And he was

hitting... along so many spots in my canal... I blinked and sucked Leander's fingers in my mouth.

Janus's cock hit... oh god, those *places*. Spots no one never talked about. Why didn't anybody ever talk about the other spots? Oh god, there was *B sharp*. Why didn't anybody ever talk about B sharp?

It was obscene. And so, so, so hot.

And I could tell, tonight was a night that Janus just needed to fuck all his demons out.

He needed to dominate me. He needed his world to make sense again. He needed a fuck toy. I didn't care to analyze why he needed what he needed but I was happy to give it to him.

"You like that you're my doll?"

I did but I didn't think he wanted me to respond. And I was okay with that.

"Good little slut," he said and spanked my ass.

He thrust in again. "You like that? You like it when Daddy fucks you so deep? I can hear by those little noises that you do. And just listen to you juicing all over my cock."

And then, while I'd had them take me hard before, Janus started fucking me like I'd never been fucked before. He started... well, just using my body like I was a hole. Like I was a doll and that was what Janus needed me to be. He was hurting and I was his object of comfort. Even if he couldn't see it, I could.

And he fucked me like a man possessed.

Until he shoved my face into the table and came deep inside me. He was rough as he yanked out and let go of my hips. "Who fucks our slut next?"

"I do," said Leander, and he sounded angry.

I tried to brace myself for another rough fuck. I could take it. My pussy was throbbing. The part of me that needed it just as much as they did was ready to be taken like this.

But when Leander came up to me, while yes, I heard his zipper go down and his buckle yank off as rough as ever...

His hands were gentle on my back. Caressing.

He couldn't have been more opposite of his brother if he tried.

Maybe he was trying. But where Janus had been so rough and dehumanizing, Leander's caresses were...*loving*.

I couldn't help the tears that flooded my eyes as he embraced me from behind and entered me so, so slow. Maybe I did need some gentle tonight after all. Easing into my sore, swollen flesh, he squeezed me to him, wrapping his arms around me. Hugging me.

"Thank you for tonight," he whispered in my ear.

And I would've sworn the twins had switched places. Who was this sweet man embracing me? I'd never seen this side of Leander before. "I'm sorry for how I've been lately," he kept whispering.

"And," he continued, "I'm a fool for not telling you before now. I love you."

Tears burst out of my eyes. He was doing this *now*, on a night of so many emotions? I hadn't even stopped to let myself process all that had been happening. Not to mention I was fucking hormonal and pregnant.

But I'd also needed this from him. Really, really needed this from him.

He slid out of me and spun me around so we were facing each other. And then he lifted me by my hips so that

I was sitting on the table. I opened my legs to him and he stepped between them, hard cock bobbing between us.

I wrapped my arms around him and he bowed his forehead to mine. "I really am sorry for being such an asshole. I have... issues sometimes. And I'm not good about talking about them. There's shit with Mom... well, you saw. It goes deep. Frankly, you scare the shit out of me and you always have." He was silent a second before finishing, "Because I knew from the beginning you could be a game changer."

I kissed him and shifted my hips forward to the edge of the table. Then I reached down for his shaft and put him inside me.

And then I wrapped my arms around his neck and for the first time maybe ever, Leander and I made love.

FIFTEEN

HOPE

THE NEXT MORNING, Milo had cooked breakfast for all of us. So I woke up to the sound of someone showering, the smell of bacon, and a warm body in bed behind me.

"Good morning, beautiful."

I turned towards the source of that husky voice. And blinked in surprise when I realized it was—

"Leander?"

Leander held my gaze. "Surprised it's me?"

I didn't say no. He reached up and pushed some hair behind my ear. "It's our last day of training today. Tomorrow, we start table reads with the rest of the cast."

I paused, happy to have a quiet moment alone with any of them considering how busy they'd all been lately.

"Is that a good thing?" I asked, fully turned towards him now. I propped myself up on my elbow.

His body was still, his gaze on me like he was thinking hard about something.

I raised my eyebrows.

"Sure, it's a good thing," he said as if there'd been no pause. But he didn't sound very convincing, or very convinced.

"Once you start filming, things will get busy, won't they?" I asked softly. I slid an arm around his waist and snuggled into him. I wanted to appreciate the *now* while I had it. Mornings sleeping in like this were already few and far between.

Leander's arm wrapped around me, embracing me back.

"Milo will be here to make sure you're taken care of."

I nodded, looking down. It was true. I loved being with Milo. I loved *Milo*. But I would also miss the twins like an ache in my bones. Yesterday I might have said some breathing room from Leander would be a good thing—

But then he'd gone and done the one thing that men usually seemed incapable of. He'd apologized and here he was the morning after, still meaning it. Not treating it like it was some drunken confession, spilled and then forgotten the next day.

It meant something.

It meant a lot to me, stupidly.

Maybe not so stupid, if I thought about it. For someone like me with a father who never once in his life could admit anything he'd done wrong...

Dad once spent three-thousand dollars on a fancy suit and then shouted at Mama and me for not having dinner on the table when there was not a single thing in the cupboard by the end of the month. And yet he would not, *could not* admit he'd made a mistake.

"Look, I wanted to say again that I'm sorry for what a jackass I've been ever since we found out about the baby," Leander said. His eyes were a luminescent silver in the morning light. "It freaked me out really badly, to tell you the truth, which is just embarrassing. But holy shit—"

He grinned and slid his hands down my forearms to clutch my hips. And then they crept back up tentatively to my stomach. "I'm going to be a father."

What the fuck was this man doing to me? Squishing my heart through the freakin' shredder, that was what.

I grinned tearily back at him and nodded. Damned hormones.

What if... What if this could actually... work? Together. Leander, Janus, and Milo. Three men and a baby. And me.

Leander pressed his forehead against mine.

Good Lord, I loved it when he did that.

Leander was a passionate man. He threw himself fully into the things he cared about. The trick was becoming something or someone he cared about. And now... was he really saying I was one of those? He finally believed me about the baby, anyway.

"What do you think about it all?" I asked. "Being a dad?"

Leander blinked. Like he was really letting himself absorb it deeply for the first time.

Damn. Maybe all his assholishness had been a defense mechanism against letting it in. If he hated and distrusted me, then he didn't have to admit he could be the father.

Shitty, yes, but then, he'd also been man enough to apologize.

Then again, I'd lived long enough to know words were one thing and actions another. So I supposed we'd see if this new Leander would stick around.

"My dad was a good guy," Leander said, blinking some more. "I mean, I think he was. He loved my mom and she loved him. I know that much."

I tilted my head. "How do you know? I mean, it's sweet, but—?"

He nodded. "Our grandpa had these old letters between them. From back when they first met in college. It was really romantic shit. Dad was even sappier than Mom. He would quote poetry. Cheesy shit." Leander laughed and breathed out at the same time, obviously recalling a memory with warmth. "And you could tell, Mom was just eating it up."

I reached out and stroked my fingers through his hair. "I think you'll be a great dad."

His breath hitched and a look of vulnerability came over his face.

The bathroom door opened and Leander ducked his face into my neck. Janus walked into the room, still naked and dripping from the shower. He used the towel to scrub his hair dry instead, naturally.

"Breakfast is ready," Milo called from the kitchen.

Leander pulled away from me, the moment between us broken. I wanted to pull him back. I wanted more.

SIXTEEN

HOPE

"HAVE you noticed a change in the guys?" I whispered to Milo as we strolled one of the long aisles of St. Anthony's Basilica.

It was one of Italy's most famous churches and was covered in frescos and statues and blah blah blah—for once, I couldn't give a shit about the history stuff.

I was the one who'd asked Milo if we could go sightseeing. But that was just because I couldn't seem to sit still back at home. Milo had his camera out—an actual camera, not just his phone—upturned to one of the many frescos overhead. We'd been sightseeing for a couple hours now. Usually I lost myself in the architecture and art as much as Milo did. But today I just couldn't stop thinking about last night and this morning...

"Hmm?" Milo asked, obviously barely listening. "Holy shit, look! We finally got to the Donatello piece."

He swung his camera around and started snapping away. We'd come on a weekday and it wasn't as flooded with tourists as it probably was on a weekend. So we could actually *see* the skinny bronze Donatello sculpture of Jesus. It hung at the apex of the central church nave.

I waited until Milo had snapped the pic before grabbing his bicep. "Could we stop looking at the ninja turtle art for a second? Leander told me he *loved* me this morning. And that was after he *apologized*."

Milo dropped his camera so that it swung on the strap around his neck, finally seeming to hear me. "Like an actual apology? Or like he implied it or something?"

I shook my head. "He said the words. Multiple times. Last night and this morning, he said he was sorry for how he's been an asshole lately."

Then I frowned. "But then Janus was the one who barely had any time for me before they left for the stables. He kept saying the jockey they were finishing training with had no patience for *American celebrity types*." I used air quotes like Janus had this morning and rolled my eyes.

"Janus doesn't like to come off as entitled," Milo said. "It embarrasses him."

"I get that, but he didn't even say goodbye. I was putting away my dish for breakfast and when I turned around, he was just gone. Usually he makes such a thing of kissing me before he leaves..."

I sighed. "Not that he has to do that every morning, or that I should let myself come to *expect* it, it was just..." I bit my lip. "It's like they've had a personality swap. Now *Janus* is the twin with an ego who's too busy to be bothered and Leander's the sensitive one?" I tossed my hands in the air.

"Shhhh!" another visitor hissed at me, crossing themselves and gesturing at Donatello's Jesus.

I dropped my eyes to the floor. And then tugged at the collar of my shirt and grabbed Milo's hand. "Let's get out of here."

Milo snapped one more picture of the Donatello sculpture and crossed himself. He was still steadfastly Greek Orthodox and crossed himself whenever we passed a church. He followed me as I hustled out.

It was sunny out, balmy and hot.

As soon as my foot touched cobblestone, I turned to Milo. "Can we go visit them? At the training stables? Janus always said we could come by. And now that I'm in my second trimester," my hand went reflexively to my tummy bump, "I finally feel good enough to go. It's the last day."

Milo only paused a second before nodding. "Sure, I'll call a car to take us out there." He pulled his phone out of his pocket.

We walked back to the hotel, stopping at a food stall for a steaming, gooey mozzarella and prosciutto panini. I'd devoured it by the time the car had Milo called arrived. I loved being able to *eat* again after the non-stop nausea first three months. I *especially* loved being able to eat again while being in *Italy*. I was licking my fingertips and wishing I'd ordered a panini to go as I climbed into the back seat with Milo.

Once we were buckled in and heading out of the city, Milo tapped his fingers on his knee like he did when he was thinking about something. Sure enough, a moment later he was talking.

"Seeing Mom brings up shit for all of us, you know." He

inclined his head towards me. "It'll probably just take a few days for things to settle back to normal."

"I hope not." My gaze strayed back to the window. The countryside was gorgeous outside the city. Gently rolling golden hills tumbled into one another. It was almost too beautiful to be believed. *Like a movie.* "I like the changes in Leander. You don't think they'll stick?" I looked back at Milo just in time to catch him shrug.

"I think him being such an asshole for so long was the weird part." Milo's eyebrows scrunched in confusion. "I mean, yeah, he and Janus give each other as good as they get. But with me and other people, usually Leander's not—"

"What?" I snapped. "He's usually *not* a cruel asshole who likes to make pregnant women cry?"

Milo cringed. "Yeah. That." He shook his head. "You know, just because he says he's sorry doesn't mean you owe him anything. You don't have to forgive him."

I nodded. It was true.

I huffed out a hard breath, slumped, and dropped my head back against the headrest. What did I think I would get by going out to the stables? That by seeing the twins in their natural habitat I'd finally somehow find the answers I was looking for?

At least I'd see some beautiful horses anyway. I giggled tiredly to myself.

I tried to focus on that, anyway. Seeing the twins, and maybe some pretty horses. I settled my hands on my belly, which had gone tight and was slowly expanding.

Such banal, useless thoughts.

I was actually *smiling*, feeling a little happy, or loose anyway.

And then the next moment an ambulance siren split the air.

Our car pulled abruptly to a stop and I shot up. We were at the stables. I pressed my hand to the glass of the window.

"What's going on?"

The ambulance passed by us on the narrow road as it roared away from the stables. I swung my head around to watch it go.

Both Milo's phone and mine started blaring at the same time. I shoved the car door open.

"Hello?" I hit the green button as I ran towards the awning of stable's entrance.

And then I started sprinting when I saw Janus standing there, looking shell-shocked with a hand on his head. In his other hand, he held a phone. "Hope?"

I barreled into him. His arms closed around me. But I yanked back almost immediately. My head swiveled as I looked around at the group of people gathered in the yard, a barn and stables in the background. "Where's Leander?"

Janus didn't immediately respond. I grabbed his arms and shook him. "Janus. Where's Leander?"

SEVENTEEN

HOPE

JANUS FINALLY CAME out of his daze when I shook him again. "What happened to Leander?"

"He fell. Or the horse threw him. I don't know, I wasn't close enough to see." Janus raked his hands through his hair. "One second we were doing our last full our run, and he went around these trees—then he was just on the ground screaming."

Janus suddenly started forward. "They wouldn't let me in the ambulance to go with him. Do you have a car?"

I nodded and jogged beside him back to where Milo was pacing beside the car. We all jumped in and Janus quickly punched the hospital into the GPS. The EMTs had given him the name before they'd driven off. He gripped the dash the whole way there, barking directions at Milo even though the GPS was doing the same thing.

"Walk us through what happened again?" I asked, even though Janus had already told us a couple times. "So he was conscious when he got on the ambulance? Or not?"

"Sort of. I don't know. Yes?" Janus shook his head. "He was going in and out of it. They had him on the stretcher."

We got to the hospital but couldn't see Leander right away because he was in surgery. *Surgery*. But no one would tell us what kind of surgery, or how bad it was, or what the *hell* was going on.

Janus was ready to tear down the walls of the place. Just when Milo was tugging him away from the nursing station before we got the Italian police called on us, my phone started blowing up with messages. And ringing. I'd silence one call and then another would start coming through.

"What the hell?" I muttered, tapping on one of the messages. It was from BuzzFeed wanting to authenticate a video that had been sent to them—of Leander getting in an accident on set.

"Son of a bitch." I blinked and then clicked the link they'd forwarded along with what was obviously a quickly spat out click-bait story.

I stared down at the screen and gasped, one hand shooting to cover my mouth as I watched shaky phone camera footage. It was a faraway shot of the field behind the stable. The footage was so grainy, it was hard to tell it was Leander as he came around the corner on his horse, other than from his recognizable shoulders and build. Not everyone was quite as intimately acquainted with him as I was, but I knew it was Leander.

And I could only watch in horror, knowing what was

coming next, as the tiny figure on the video looked over his shoulder behind him and then he swung back around front—

I blinked and Leander was just flying through the air.

Wait, what happened? The horse didn't even rear up or stumble—

I fumbled with my finger to drag the dot on the *play* bar back to the beginning, determined not to look away or blink for even a second this time.

"What's that?" Milo said from behind me, phone in hand. "Are you getting all these messages too? I don't know how they found out about the accident so fast."

I shushed him with a waved hand as I pushed play again.

He looked over my shoulder at the screen as Leander came flying around the corner again. He had good stature, was well-placed in the saddle, and looked in full control of the horse.

Then he glanced back over his shoulder, looked forwards again, and then—

I brought the phone closer and squinted so I wouldn't miss the next moment. But like before it all happened so fast.

Milo gasped when the dark shape—Leander's body— flew off the horse. "Fuck!"

I could only blink as the image started bouncing up and down—probably as whoever was holding the camera ran to help. But the feed cut off before they actually got to Leander.

"Did you see what I just saw?" Milo asked, bewildered.

"What?" I looked up at him.

"Did it look like—" He shook his head but continued anyway. "I don't know. Like he just sorta... *let go* of the horse and went limp before he fell?"

"What do you mean? That he *let* himself fall? What are you even talking about?"

Milo just shrugged and looked at the floor. "Never mind. I'm sure I'm wrong."

"I finally got his room number," Janus said, coming over to us in a rush. "He's not out of surgery yet, but I finally got to someone who actually knows how to do their job—" Janus flashed a frustrated gaze back at the guy manning the nursing station. Milo pulled Janus further away by his elbow when the guy frowned at us.

"Okay, so where do we go?" I asked. "And did you find anything out about his condition?"

"I made some calls," Janus said as he strode down the hospital corridor as if he knew where he was going. "And I got hold of the hospital administrator. I mentioned that once paparazzi find out a celebrity is here, they'll be crushing the place. And if I have negative things to say about my brother's hospital stay, there will be only too many willing cameras to listen to what I have to say."

"They're already circling," Milo said as we hurried to keep up with Janus. "Someone leaked the story. And footage of the fall."

"Mother-fucking vultures," Janus spat. We took the stairs to the second floor instead of the elevator, probably because Janus had too much nervous energy to burn off.

He didn't slow down once we got to the second floor,

either. He just kept on striding as if he knew the hospital inside and out, only once having to go back and retrace his steps. It was clear he was done asking for help, directions, or anything else that might hinder him from getting to his brother any quicker.

He only slowed once he came to the big wing of the hospital labeled, *Chirurgia,* and in smaller letters underneath in English, *Surgery*.

Janus walked up to the attendant at a desk there. "Leander Mavros," he said. "I was told I could get an update on my brother here."

The woman looked up at all of us a little startled. But then she held up a finger and reached for the telephone. She picked up the headset, pushed a button, and spoke rapid Italian into the phone. Then she set it down, smiled and again put up one finger.

"I don't want to wait," Janus growled out. "I *want* to see my brother."

"Just chill a sec," I said to him. If he threw a shit-fit here, we wouldn't get any information.

And a couple of minutes later—right before Janus's top was about to blow—a skinny middle-aged doctor came out of a door and walked up to us.

"You are the brother?" the man asked in heavily accented English.

Janus nodded. "How is he? How did the surgery go? What was the surgery even *for?*"

"Give him space to take a breath." I knocked Janus in the side.

He looked at me and I could see how frustrated he was.

But the doctor soon began to speak. "His leg is broken in two places." He rapidly reeled off a bunch of jargon I couldn't follow, likely even if half of the terms weren't Italian—but I got the jist that Janus's ankle was seriously broken.

"We operated and put in a rod and three screws," he summarized helpfully at the end.

"Holy shit," Milo swore.

"Is he gonna be okay?" I asked.

The doctor smiled, but it was gentle. "He is put back together again, but he is in pain."

"Will he be able to walk?" Janus asked.

The smile left the doctor's face and he held up his hand in a so-so gesture. "With time. *Fisioterapia*."

"Physical therapy?" Janus repeated, features going tense. "How much? How long?"

The doctor again didn't seem to want to make promises. "Eight weeks. A few months."

"Months?" Janus said, eyes popping wide. "We don't have months! He's supposed to start shooting a movie *tomorrow*."

"Hey, we just found out he's okay," Milo said, reaching out a hand to Janus's shoulder. "Let's focus on that."

"Can we see him?" Janus shrugged Milo off.

The doctor shook his head. "He woke up once after surgery but then fell asleep again. And he needs his rest. But when he wakes, a nurse come for you."

"Can't we just sit with him?" I asked, taking a tiny step towards the doctor. "Please? Then he'd at least be able to wake up to friendly faces."

The doctor narrowed his eyes at me. Not unkindly, just with professional curiosity. "You are—?"

"Family," Janus said. "And this is my other brother." He slapped Milo on the back and then stared down the doctor. "Your hospital administrator talked do you, right? Tommaso? Because he said he would take care of *whatever* we needed." Janus leaned in, eyebrow lifting significantly. "Considering how we might be feeling generous to the hospital in response? With our charity donations?"

The doctor listened to all this warily, then looked towards the small reception area. He spoke in rapid Italian to the receptionist, then nodded back at us. "Come. I will show you his room."

AND SO BEGAN our hours-long vigil at Leander's bedside, long into the night. His face was angelic in spite of a nasty bruise on the right side of his jaw. He'd obviously fallen hard on that side; it was his right leg he'd broken too. It was wrapped in a plaster cast up to his thigh and lifted high in traction.

An IV line pierced his arm and he was so pale...so ghastly pale compared to his usual vibrant glow. For once, he and Janus didn't look like twins. Or if they did, Leander seemed a ghostly echo of his hale and healthy brother. Janus was standing beside Leander's bed but wasn't touching him.

I sat on a chair on the opposite side of Leander, clutching his cold hand. I didn't understand how Janus could simply stand there like he was keeping guard, cold and aloof. I wanted to yell at him to take Leander's other hand.

Milo had spent the last forty-five minutes talking Leander's ear off—no matter that he was unconscious—before finally de-camping to go get some coffee for all of us.

But Janus hadn't said a single word to his brother.

My irritation finally spilled over. "Say something," I prompted. "It will do him good to hear your voice."

But Janus just scoffed mirthlessly. "It's his own voice. Why the fuck would he want to hear his own voice? You talk."

I shook my head at him in frustration but started talking anyway. I wanted Leander to have a voice to walk towards through the darkness.

Maybe we ought to let him sleep, but I figured we all just needed to see that he was okay firsthand. Then I could let myself try to catch a nap on the little cot they'd arranged for us to take turns sleeping in. Because none of us were leaving Leander alone until we had a better handle on the situation. Janus's promised donation had at least gotten us an exemption from visiting hours, thank God. I didn't like how wealth opened doors, but I couldn't say I wasn't grateful in this situation.

"Leander?" I said, my voice coming out rough from worry and the quiet crying I'd been doing all afternoon and evening. "I'm sorry I didn't say it back this morning. And maybe it's shit to say it here while you aren't even conscious..."

I squeezed his hand. "But I love you too." The memory of his body flying off the horse in the video flashed in my mind. What had he been thinking in that moment? People broke their spines in horse riding accidents every day. People *died*.

I swallowed back a choked breath. "You know that, right? You know I love you?"

"Of course I know," came Leander's scratchy voice as his eyes cracked open just the slightest bit. "Now what the fuck does it take to get some water around here?"

PART 2

EIGHTEEN

LEANDER

MY LEG. It was bad.

Really fuckin' bad.

They'd had to install a rod in my tibia and screws in my ankle. At least that was what I thought I'd heard the doctor say. I was kind of in and out of it from the painkillers.

In my brief windows of consciousness that first day, Hope was there every time I opened my eyes. She was beautiful. So beautiful it hurt. Okay, so maybe that was my goddamned leg.

But when she'd looked down at where I was laid out, her hands curving around her tummy like they did now unconsciously whenever she was worried... Protecting our kid. My damn *kid*, tiny as a grape or however the fuck big the fetus was now.

My eyes—the only part of my body that didn't hurt, it

seemed like—moved to Janus who was pacing back and forth behind her.

Back and forth, back and forth. He was my mirror image, hovering like a ghost by my bedside. It was funny, I'd grown up so used to seeing him that it was looking in the mirror that made me jump sometimes. Like he'd snuck up on me when I thought I was alone. And yet that was the one thing neither of us had ever managed to be, was it? To be alone without the other.

Well, maybe it was time for that to change.

I struggled to hold my eyes open as the sun set. The hospital administrator had moved me to a room on the top floor. Drawn shades covered the window, but natural light still spilled through. Milo sat on a chair in the corner, thumbs moving on his phone screen. He'd been on the phone almost nonstop today.

The studio wanted answers about their latest cash cow that was currently frozen in production.

After sitting vigil at my bedside all afternoon long, Hope finally left the room for a bathroom break. I quickly snapped my brother's name. "Janus."

He'd been quiet all day, barely talking to me. That was fine—talking wasn't necessary. We were too close. I knew his mind, as much as he might hate the fact. But I was also counting on it.

"Tell Milo to call the studio back. Tell them you'll take the role in my place."

Janus's eyes went wide. "What the fuck are you talking about? They're already quietly making inquiries for someone else to fill in."

"Some people are calling the movie cursed," Milo

muttered. He'd come up behind him, still looking down at his phone. "Two actors dropping out of the same lead role, one after the other."

"So don't," I said, gritting my teeth against the pulsing pain in my leg. I wasn't gonna take any more pain meds until I cleared this up, but I couldn't hold out much longer. I'd just been waiting for Hope to leave so I could have this conversation. "No one has to know how bad this accident really was. Janus, you've been prepping for this. So step up."

Janus froze, gray eyes locked with mine. Milo had also paused.

"I can't." Janus shook his head.

I reached out and snatched his wrist, even though the motion made me wince. "You can. And you will. We need this."

His eyes widened. I could tell the idea was sinking in. In fact, I could tell it wasn't an entirely new concept.

He'd been considering it as a solution too. As much as we were different, we were also too alike. We had similar interests. Similar tastes in hobbies. Similar tastes in women... It was part of what made it so insufferable to live with one another.

"I don't have the time or energy to debate," I barked. "Just say yes like you know you want to."

Janus pulled his arm away from my grasp. Still staring straight at me. Doing the thing where we silently communicated. *What are you doing?*

What needs to be done. You know it does.

More silent staring.

Fine.

But then Janus leaned down, surprising me. "What the fuck happened out there? You were riding fine, then I come around the bend and—"

He stared at me, obviously waiting for me to fill in the blank.

"And then I fell," I said, glaring him down.

"You fell," he repeated. A beat of silence. "Just like that?"

"Just like that."

"Did the horse get spooked? Rear up or something?"

Milo piped up from behind him. "I saw the video. It didn't look like the horse reared up."

"Let's let *him* tell us what happened." Janus's eyes skewered me. "The truth this time."

"I've been telling you the truth." I didn't let a muscle twitch. "I fell off the damn horse. We all saw the video. I'm on the horse. Then I'm not."

Janus started shaking his head but just then Hope came back in through the door. She looked startled to see Janus and Milo crouched over the bed talking to me.

"What'd I miss?" she asked, bright and curious.

"Nothing," I said loudly. "I was just talking to them about arrangements for when I get out of here tomorrow."

"Tomorrow?" she said, immediately looking worried. One hand went to rub her belly and I smiled. Fuck, she was beautiful. Perfect, actually, even if I'd been too blind to see it at first. Then I frowned. All this stress couldn't be good for the baby.

"You should go back to the hotel," I said.

Hope immediately started shaking her head. "I'm fine. That's what the cot—"

I lifted up off the bed in spite of the pain. "You are pregnant with my child and you will *not* sleep on a fucking c—"

"Whoa, whoa, there," Milo said, putting hands on my shoulder and shoving me back down to the mattress. "Down, cowboy."

I glared at Milo. "Our pregnant..." I searched for the right word, finally growling, "*woman,*" when it was the only one I could come up with, "is not sleeping on a shitty canvas cot that looks about two seconds from falling apart. Take her back to the apartment."

"I'm not leaving you—" Hope started.

"He's not wrong," Janus cut in, brows narrowing uncertainly. His eyes zeroed in on her thickening tummy. Finally, someone seeing sense around here.

It took several more minutes of Hope huffing and getting more and more red-faced before she realized she was fighting a losing battle. The three of us were determined she get some actual rest.

She finally came towards me and jammed a finger in my chest. "Fine. I'll go. But first I need to tell you something." She crossed her arms over her bosoms. "Just you."

The pain in my leg was pulsing again, bad, but I was too curious. Now that I'd let myself see the woman in front of me for all that she was, I couldn't get enough of her.

So I waved my brothers to get lost. "Give us the room. Don't you have some calls to be making anyway?" I gave Janus a significant look. His eyes flitted to Hope, but then he nodded and he and Milo left.

Hope breathed out as soon as the door closed behind them. Then she walked over to it and flipped the lock. I raised an eyebrow as she turned back around towards me.

"You scared the shit outta me today," she whispered. Machines hummed in the room and somewhere there was a slow *beep beep beep* of my heartbeat. She walked back towards me, and as she came, she grasped the hem of her shirt and in one quick sweep, lifted it up and off over her head.

Her gorgeous breasts were exposed. Like large, luscious melons, barely enclosed in the half-shelf lacy-bra she wore.

I blinked, my mind going blank for a second.

Especially when she continued forward. Her fingernails, filed and glossy, trailed down my chest and gripped the top of the blanket covering me. My breath hiccupped as she tugged the blanket down. Then she lifted my hospital gown up. The *beep beep beep* of my heartbeat on the machine was suddenly speeding up rapidly.

"Hope, I—"

She grinned at me, and I fucking loved her in this moment for not pitying me. For treating me like a whole man as she gripped my cock that had quickly hardened and dragged it towards her open mouth.

"Oh fuck," I groaned as she flicked the very tip of my dick with her wicked little tongue.

"I love you," she whispered.

And then she bent over and swallowed me whole.

Fuck it, this was the best kind of pain-reliever there was. My hand without an IV in it lifted just enough to curl my fingers in her long, thick hair.

When she lifted up, my whole body tensed. *Fuck*, that hurt my leg. But pleasure spiked down my spine at the same time.

Goddamned witch, did she know she was blowing me

and my goddamned mind at the same time with this mix of pleasure and pain?

The way she grabbed my balls and bobbed so low on my cock she was swallowing me—

My fingers grabbed hard in her hair. Fuck. Her throat felt just like her pussy. Hot and wet and tight—

Then she started humming. Growling and groaning on my cock. And when I looked down at her, the hand not propping herself up against the bed was reaching down for her own sex.

She was touching herself. While she deep-throated me.

My woman.

That was all I could call her. My woman, and barely that. *If* that. I'd fucked things up so royally. Then freaked out and fucked things up even *worse* when she told me she was pregnant. When I was in danger of losing everything, losing her—

She swallowed and applied such suction that— Oh fuck — Oh fucking fuck, holy—

I wrenched up off the bed again. Pain shot like goddamned lightning through my leg.

My hips jutted up and I came like a freight train down the throat of the most beautiful fucking woman on the entire fucking planet.

And prayed like fuck that she'd give me a *third* chance. Because I *wouldn't* let her down this time—

NINETEEN

JANUS

THE TABLE-READ TODAY WENT GREAT.
Exhilarating, even.

And I didn't know how the fuck to feel about that.

My brother was back home in bed with his leg all but in
fucking traction. Hope and Milo were there with him. And
I'd been here all day. With a famous director and co-stars.

Living a dream.

And lying to everyone. Like always.

Leander convinced Hope to go along with it. I'm not
sure how he did that. I thought she'd be reluctant. It was
one of the reasons I hadn't wanted to bring up what I
thought was a pretty obvious solution to everyone's prob-
lems since Leander had become sidelined. Well, that and I
thought it was self-aggrandizing and maybe ludicrous to
suggest myself for the job. Especially right after my
brother just had a fucking terrifying injury—I mean, only a

mercenary asshole would think about work at a time like that...

... So what did that make me?

But then Hope came out of the hospital room a couple nights ago, and she had a little smile on her face. She agreed to everything we said. And I realized she was glad that there was a solution that took the stress off of Leander. Which made *me* glad. Of course he should be our focus.

When I woke up yesterday morning, Hope had done her work. The headlines were already being blasted—initial reports that Leander Mavros were hurt on set had been mistaken. It was actually his twin brother *Janus* who'd been gravely injured.

Hope sounded so convincing as she sold the story we artfully crafted for the media. *Leander was just fine and on track to begin filming. There was simply confusion while Leander took time off to be with his brother right after the accident.*

So today I'd shown up for the table-read. Photos were taken and posted all over socials to prove that "Leander" was hale, healthy, and at work.

And for once, I wasn't just posing for the photos and then getting up to exchange places while Leander did the real work.

I'd pretended to be my brother a lot in the last decade, but this took it to a whole new level. It mingled the lines between reality and fiction in a way I couldn't quite wrap my head around. Because when I read the script for the table-read, I wasn't *playing* Leander playing the character.

It was just me. Janus. Just me and my skill or lack of it.

And no one batted an eye. No one on the cast or crew

had known Leander beforehand. So I could be myself and just... lose myself in the process. Lose myself in what I'd grown up loving to do.

I'd felt lighter than air as a driver brought me home. I jogged up the stairs instead of taking the elevator. I wanted to go in, wrap my arms around my woman, and hoist her in the air. Then drag her to bed.

But when I finally put my key in the lock, and pushed inside, the apartment was dim. I was about to call out to see if anyone was home, but then I heard distant voices. Likely from the back bedroom where Leander was. It sounded like both Milo and Hope were back there with him.

When I'd left early this morning, Milo had been helping Hope drag a couple big chairs from the living room in there to set up a makeshift office. So Leander wouldn't have to be alone.

Guilt cut through my stomach.

I wanted to go join them all. I even walked down the hallway. But I paused just outside the door. I wanted to go in and tell Hope about my day. I wanted to tell her about how bizarre it had all felt. But also how natural. How I didn't know what the right thing to do was anymore.

I'd been so sure of every move I was making just a week ago.

My path had been so clear. I was building the family I'd always wanted. Craved, even.

I swallowed uncomfortably, my hand on the doorknob to enter Leander's room. Hope's bell-like laughter rang out.

Leander was making her laugh. Last week things had been so tense between them they could only hate fuck and now she was laughing at his jokes?

Just because the motherfucker happened to tumble off a horse and break some bones?

I was the one she'd said yes to marrying. And while chances might be slim, it was still possible it was my kid she was carrying in there. She loved *me* and I loved her. Everything was going my way.

So why did all this feel like déjà vu? I blinked, took a breath, and my hand fell away from the doorknob.

I knew why.

This wasn't the first time my brother had snatched away everything I wanted right when it was all at my fingertips.

Anger started to build, only to be swept away by another wave of guilt.

Leander's leg was broken in multiple places. He was in terrible pain because he was trying hard to avoid taking the pain meds. After our teenage years, we'd both sworn off pills and drugs in all forms. He was in pain and struggling. Not to mention that he'd given *me* the role of a lifetime.

We need this, he'd said. Like we were a united front after all. So why was I still treating it like we were enemies pitted against each other? Just out of habit? Because Mom had been doing that to us since we were kids?

'Cause our childhood was fucked up. Maybe it took me too long to see it. But I did now. You could try as hard as possible to follow the rules but it didn't matter. The rules always changed. There was no way to be good enough for Mom.

But still I'd lived for her praise. When I was a kid, she'd take whichever of us had managed to get the most screen-time on *Who's Counting Now* that week out for ice cream. She had the ability to make you feel so special. Then after we got home from ice cream, she'd take you to rewatch tape of yourself. And she'd critique your acting and tell you what you should do better. There was never a reward without a stick. As fucking twisted Mommy Dearest as it all was...

To a kid who'd lost his parents when he was too young to remember, it felt like... ya know. Love.

Milo had insisted she was evil. Manipulative. And I'd tried to deny it all these years.

Leander called her a narcissist. He detailed the symptoms of the personality condition and then reminded me of times Mom had shown examples of every single one.

And I'd known they weren't totally wrong. But no one was perfect, I'd told myself. Yeah, I'd figured, Mom had been trying to re-live some of her glory days through us. She'd never made it as an actress, so she wanted to live vicariously through her kids. What was so wrong with that? Lots of people did. It was called leaving a legacy. Wasn't that why people had kids?

That was all the bullshit I'd been spinning to myself all these years, at least.

Until suddenly it was possible *I* might have a kid.

Then that woman shows up and treats us like that?

I'd move fuckin' heaven and earth for that little seedling in Hope's belly, and yet the woman who called herself our mother could only come see us when there was something she could get out of it for herself? In other words, we were just things to use. And we always had been.

Even when we were fucking *kids*.

It took me all these years to see our mother for what she was. Controlling. Conniving. Mercenary. I'd refused to see it. I'd been so sure everyone else was wrong. That I was right. My way was the right way. The only way.

... So how was I different from her? It had always been *her* way or the highway.

I pulled away from the door and stepped back.

Call time was early in the morning. Maybe I should just go shower and hit the sack. Leander was right, anyway. We needed this and I couldn't fuck it up by not being rested. They were all counting on me.

So I backed silently down the hallway and headed to my own room instead.

TWENTY

HOPE

IT FELT wrong to call the next weeks some of the best of my life. Leander was in such pain. And we barely saw Janus, he was working so much. Rehearsal schedule had been pretty nonstop and now that they'd actually started *filming,* it would be even worse. Apparently twelve-hour days were the usual. Milo and I were also working long hours to manage media coverage along with keeping the secret of which twin was actually on set.

Not to mention handling the continuing publicity of Leander's last movie and all the hype of filming the current one. And handling the twins' socials, which they'd finally caved about and let me start up again. Just Instagram. Not too invasive. Only pics of the set and around Italy. Enough to satisfy fans and keep "Leander" on their radar without getting too private.

Meanwhile, the real Leander *was* healing. Getting out

of bed to get to the bathroom was getting easier. He usually needed Milo's help, but in the beginning, he'd needed *both* of our help.

Yesterday during a long afternoon, when we'd watched as much streaming TV as we could stand, he'd clicked off the TV.

"Oh, the baby's moving again." I yawned and put a hand to my stomach. It was the weirdest thing when I'd first felt it. Like when you had a muscle spasm, except it was inside my stomach. Like a fluttering.

Leander all but launched himself off the bed to get to me so he could press his hand against my stomach. The butterflies feeling had already stopped and I laughed at him, half in-half-out of the bed, his leg still perched awkwardly on the several pillows as he reached for my belly.

"It's stopped," I said, urging him back on to the bed.

"Tell me sooner next time."

"I still barely know when I'm feeling it!" I laughed. "And the book says it'll still be a long time till you can feel it from the outside." I'd been smiling all week because of it. If the little bean was moving, then they were healthy.

Leander winced as he got back into the bed. Milo was out doing some shopping so I hopped out of my chair by the bed up to help him settle back in.

"Are you in pain? Do you need help shifting?"

He just shook his head as he rearranged himself.

"Are you hungry? I could pop out and get something."

Another shake of the head.

"Are you sure? Or I could get a snack from the kitchen?"

"I'm fine."

"Really, it's not a problem, I can just—"

"Hope. Stop. Just stop. For one second stop running around trying to fix everything. And everyone. You're pregnant. You need a break too."

I paused, taken aback. The first week he'd been quite groggy before he got stricter about cutting down the pain meds. Last week he'd just wanted to be distracted, though he was easily irritated by Milo and anytime Janus came by. So we'd played games. Crosswords.

This week he'd been different still, going much quieter. Internal. He just wanted the TV on... though I caught him staring at the wall most of the time instead of watching. I wasn't sure it was a good or bad sign, so I'd been trying to be extra considerate.

But when he reached over and interlaced his fingers with mine, I was more surprised still.

"Just sit here with me for a while?" he asked. "No TV, no distractions?"

"Oh." I blinked as he squeezed my hand with his. It was so nice. "Okay."

A small smile graced his lips. "I really appreciate all you've been doing for me. I'm sorry I haven't said so before now. I know I'm not the best patient."

"You're fine," I said. "You're doing amazing. Really."

He looked towards the window and the smile dropped from his face. "Am I? I've been having a lot of time to think about things. Kinda hard to avoid when you're stuck in bed twenty-four-seven. I know you'll be shocked to hear this," he chuckled, his voice low and husky, "but I don't always handle my, uh, emotions the best."

I felt my eyes widen. Wow. He was really going there? Afraid I'd say the wrong thing, I just nodded.

"Mom never really... I mean, the reason we were such good actors was because kids mirror their parents. And she just..." He shook his head, rubbing his thumb over this several days of scruff on his chin. "She was so natural at having two faces—the one she showed everyone else, and the one she had at home. So of course Janus, Milo, and I were all natural actors. As kids we did the same thing she was doing, except we did it to please her. Reacting to her, walking on eggshells to try to make her happy, learning to be just as gymnastic as she was with our moods."

I nodded even though my chest hurt at hearing it. "I'm so sorry."

I climbed up onto the bed beside him, ever so careful not to disturb his leg. "I know a little bit about what that's like. I could never be myself around my dad. He expected me to be a certain way and if I wasn't like that... Well, I don't know. I never tried anything else until I left. And then I didn't know who I was. I was just this blank slate of carved-out pieces—what I'd tried to be for him my whole life." I looked back up at him after a pause. "What was it like for you?"

His jaw was hard. "I hate that for you."

I nodded. "I'm figuring it out. *Way too late*. Embarrassingly late. You and Milo and Janus have been helping me with the last few pieces. But I'm sure it was different for you. As a guy and without the religious stuff."

He squeezed my hand again. "I don't know. A toxic, controlling parent is still gonna mess you up one way or another."

I nodded.

"As a teenager, I thought I knew everything," he continued, just when I thought he wouldn't. I was so surprised because this was just when Janus would have closed up. He only ever revealed tidbits at a time, but Leander was really opening up to me.

"I thought I was so fucking cool, and adult, because I hung around adults all the time." He shook his head, rolling his eyes at himself, "But I was still a kid. And I still just wanted my mom to love me and give me the time of day."

"God, Leander, I'm so sorry—"

He waved my words away, so I stopped to let him talk.

"I'm just trying to explain," he said. "I thought I was rebelling. I thought I was so grown up. I thought doing drugs and having sex with one of my older female producers even though I was just a teenager meant I was the shit. That I was proving anything other than what a dumb, selfish little fuck I was."

He blew out a long breath, jaw still clenched. He was clearly furious at his younger self.

My stomach twisted. I'd seen so much predatory behavior and grooming of teen girls during my time in the industry, so many men called out for bad behavior. So I wasn't shocked to see the reverse, as much as it sickened me.

"Hey." I reached out and pushed some hair back from his forehead. He needed a haircut. "You were just a kid. You said so yourself."

His gaze shot to mine. "I was still old enough to know better."

I scoffed. "How? How old were you?"

His jaw went so hard it seemed in danger of shattering. I squeezed his hand again.

"Seventeen."

"That's child abuse!"

He shrugged.

"You were a kid! Give me the bitch's name." I was already reaching out for my phone, infuriated. "I'll get her blacklisted."

"She's not in show business anymore. I saw to it once *Gemini* started blowing up."

I breathed out, fury still bubbling underneath my skin. These boys. This fucking parasitic system had used and abused them since the time they were *children*. No one who was supposed to look out for them had. Everyone was just happy that the boys were able to keep producing on screen. *Who's Counting Now* had huge ratings at the end of its run, in part *because* of the boys' teenage character Dylan.

I was ashamed to have been such a fan when there was so much going on behind the scenes I hadn't known about. Their horrible mother. Some abusive producer harming Leander behind the scenes because she was some sick fuck. I wanted to scream at the fucking world sometimes.

Instead, I cradled my slightly protruding stomach. More than ever, I wanted to protect this child from all that the world could do to them.

"We'll do everything different," I said passionately. "We'll protect them." I grasped Leander's hand and pressed it to my belly.

"Are they moving?" he asked excitedly, apparently forgetting our upsetting conversation.

I shook my head. "But I have the appointment tomorrow. We'll get to hear the baby's heartbeat again." I couldn't help grinning at that.

Leander insisted on coming along the next day, though I knew it had to be painful to be upright for several hours on that leg. Not to mention the unpleasant trip there. He hadn't had to use his crutches so extensively since the painful trip home from the hospital, and at least then he'd been on painkillers. But he was determined, in spite of the sheen of sweat that broke out across his forehead by the time we got there.

Since Janus had started filming this week, there was just no way he could take off—especially when he was supposed to be Leander. If anyone found out I was pregnant, at least it made sense for "Janus," my fiancé, to be with me when I went to the doctor.

I was starting to show. Right now my tummy could be written off as a summer of eating Italian food... Which, granted, I had been indulging. Ever since the nausea had passed, I *had* been stuffing myself with fresh homemade pasta and pizza and the most delicious carbs on the *planet*, in the place where they had been perfected.

There was this one little hole in the wall restaurant where there was a trio of ancient Italian women who literally *made* the pasta and oh my *God*, the parmigiana sauce they made. I went there every single afternoon last week for lunch.

I'd been plump before, but now I was positively rounding out. And my boobs! Sheesh. My bras had quickly become a joke. I'd forced Milo to go bra shopping for me because I didn't want to leave Leander's side.

"You ready?"

Thankfully, they had water in a little cooler in the office. I brought two for Leander. He was sweating from the hot August day, and I could only imagine the extra heat a thigh-high cast added.

We had to wait half an hour in the waiting room but they finally called us back. I'd only had the one other appointment before this, so at least I was somewhat familiar with the drill. I laid back and the nurse technician lifted my shirt to coat my belly with cold gel.

Immediately, a strong heartbeat started rapidly *whoosh whoosh whooshing* over the machine's speaker. Even though I felt the bean swimming around in there most days, it was still more than a relief to hear that little heartbeat pounding away.

"Oh!" the nurse, who spoke fluent English, exclaimed as a picture began to show on the little screen.

Last time it had just been a black and white image and I'd barely been able to see what the nurse had been pointing to.

This one was different—flesh-colored organs, sacs, and bubbles flashed by on screen—but I still couldn't tell what I was looking at. "It's so funny when their heartbeats get in sync like that," the nurse said.

I frowned. "What do you mean?"

"The babies," the nurse said, and I thought maybe she was just flubbing the plural because of the language difference.

But then she slowed down the ultrasound wand on my belly. "See, here is the first baby." She pointed at the screen and I could see the vague outline of a head and a tiny little rapidly thumping heart. Then she shifted the wand. "And the second baby."

"Second baby?" Leander's voice was an octave higher than usual.

The nurse technician looked down at the chart. "Did you not know you were having twins?"

TWENTY-ONE

LEANDER

"TWINS!" Janus whooped over the phone which Hope had to her ear but I could still hear anyway. "Shut the front door! Dammit, I wanna get home and squeeze you." His voice lowered. "And more. Fuck, I miss you."

My leg hurt like a son-of-a-bitch from being on it for multiple hours, and sorry-not-sorry, I didn't have time for my whiny-ass brother at the moment. I grabbed the phone out of Hope's hand. "Yeah, it's amazing. 'Kay, see ya later, bro."

I tossed the phone on the side table right inside the foyer. "Milo, get her into the bedroom," I gritted out through the pain screaming up my leg. "Now."

"Hey! I was talking to him. And you need to get off that leg!" Hope said, wagging a finger in my face even as Milo started manhandling her towards the bedroom. "You've been grimacing for the past half hour!" Her voice echoed back towards me down the hallway.

"I won't say no to creative pain relief." I grimaced as I hobbled behind them on my crutches.

When I got to the doorway, it was to find my curvaceous, juicy woman standing in the doorway, one hip popped, leg out. The extra swell of her belly shouldn't be so erotic. But knowing she was growing my progeny...

"Yes, Daddy," she said, biting her bottom lip. "I wanna play."

Well, fuck.

"Flip her and bend her against the bed," I growled to Milo.

Milo was apparently ready too, dragging Hope by the hips and bending her face first over the foot of the bed. Then he yanked down her stretchy leggings and lace underwear in anticipation for what came next.

I hobbled into the room, the front of my pants quickly growing tight. And my pain began to recede as the thing I was focused most on shifted.

"Fuck, I love these cheeks." I reached down and grabbed Hope's very large, *very luscious* ass. Her cheeks were so sweet and round. Leaning on one crutch, I smacked her ass and breathed out as it jiggled. My cock went fully hard as she wriggled back and forth on her feet, making her flesh undulate even more.

Goddamn, I loved her body.

I couldn't reach down and undo the button of my jeans fast enough. Still annoyingly slow because I had to balance myself, wincing in pain. But I got the job done. And it was sweet release to let my iron-hard shaft free. My hand trembled as I reached down to touch those oh-so-soft, jiggly ass cheeks.

Ever so slowly, fucking reverently, I thrust my bare cock forwards into the dark nest between her legs. I'd never admit it out loud, but one of the best fucking perks about her being pregnant was the ability to bareback her without any hesitation at all. No fears in the back of my mind. Well, there were so many perks. Her sweet curves had rounded out even more. Her breasts were *insane*...

All because she was already carrying my child...no, Jesus, my *children*. Two babies. Holy fuck. I couldn't quite wrap my head around it and yet I was stupid happy at the same time. Happier than I could ever remember feeling, now that I'd allowed myself to let it in.

A real family. Ready-made for me.

If I didn't let it slip through my grasp.

I leaned into Hope, inhaling the fruit-fragrant scent of her neck. Fucking peaches or some shit. I pulled out of her, enjoying every inch of the slide, and groaned as I thrust back in again. Hope's bare, tight little pussy clenched me so good.

She reached back around and dug her fingernails into my hair. "*Daddy*," she groaned. Her sex clenched hard around me, still so fucking wet. Like fucking heaven on my bare cock. Oh fuck, I'd never get used to it. Oh *fuuuuuuck*—

I jerked forwards again, my pelvis to her plump ass. A sheen of sweat covered my chest. With my one free hand I clenched her hip. I fucking loved this spot on her body, right where her waist flared out to her hips and ass. Where her feminine softness rounded to welcome my hardness.

I slapped her ass and she clenched around me again as

her flesh jiggled. I thrust hard and my balls slapped her pussy.

Fuck, that was so goddamned satisfying. I stretched forwards with my hips, bottoming out inside her but being careful not to thrust too hard against her cervix. I still rolled and explored every inch inside of her with the head of my cock. The doctor said sex was safe (Hope was the one who'd asked), and that a moderate level of exercise was even good. So I wanted to make sure she felt me. By her low groan, I could tell she did.

"Come in," I said to Milo. "Reach around. You can rub her clit while you jerk off."

I'd seen him in the periphery doing his thing—watching us and getting the fuck off like the kinky bastard he was. I didn't have enough hands free at the moment, so Milo would have to step up like he had at the beginning.

And he got to it quick enough, between Hope and the bed, down, down. I felt his hand there, pressing Hope's swollen clit and pussy lips against my shaft as I thrust in and out of her.

And Hope started freaking the fuck out beneath me.

"Oh God, oh God!" she cried. She let go of my hair and scrambled for the quilt for stability. Her sex clenched and spasmed on my cock as she came.

Her thick, dimpled ass essentially bounced up and down, twerking on my dick.

Fuck. Oh fuck.

Every goddamn thought leaked outta my head.

Power built at the base of my spine. Pressure. Goddamn. I fucked her. She kept coming. Fucking harder. Goddamn. I squeezed her ass. Spanked her. Fucked her.

My cock was hard as marble. Hard as fucking diamonds.

I fucked my baby's sweet little cunt, pinning Milo's hand against her swollen clit and making her scream.

She was mine.

My family.

My forever.

I bent down and sunk my teeth into the back of her neck as her cunt milked me. I fucked out my release deep into her pussy.

TWENTY-TWO

JANUS

IT'S NOT FAIR. I loved her first.

Tonight I came in late, at two a.m. Still, I thought maybe just maybe, I'd catch everyone still up for a late night... snack.

But the apartment was quiet. Silent and dark. Usually Hope was careful to leave a lamp on for me, but maybe she fell asleep in bed watching TV again. I heard from Milo she had been doing that a lot lately. He was my inside man who helped keep me updated beyond whatever stolen moments I could manage to facetime Hope on filming breaks.

A lot of times when I called midday lately, I couldn't get ahold of her because she was napping. Apparently, growing humans was exhausting.

Milo said he found her asleep on the toilet the other day!

God, it sounded adorable.

I couldn't believe I spent the last decade on the sidelines missing the stage so bad... and then now the one time I *wanted* to be sidelined, Leander breaks his leg and I have to fill in working eighteen-hour days. There were a couple days last week I didn't even bother coming back from set in Venice because considering travel time, it would've been pointless to make the roundtrip to Padua and back. And as much as I might like to deny it, I needed sleep too.

So it was probably better the house was quiet. For once, my call time wasn't till seven tomorrow. I could get a solid five hours, minus a shower.

I sighed out hard, sneaking down towards the hallway to push open the door. And there they all were. In spite of Leander's leg, the three of them were snuggled up together on the bed. Hope in the middle. Leander on the left, Milo on the right.

And a partridge in a pear tree.

Apparently, things were running smoother than ever without me.

Hope shifted in her sleep and I thought I might have wakened her. But she just nestled into Leander's chest. She let out an adorable little snort and Milo turned into her body, spooning her from behind.

They looked like a perfect little family. Complete.

So where did *I* fit in anymore?

I guess maybe it wasn't Leander's fault for always seeming so aloof when he was filming. It was fucking impossible to be anything but with a schedule like this. But then, he always pushed everyone away before they could even get close. *I* was the one trying to build us a family, to put down any kind of roots and give us *some* semblance of normalcy, as much as any of us had ever known.

Except now the woman of *my* dreams was cozied up in *their* arms.

I breathed slow and backed out, shutting the door as quietly as possible behind me. Again. I could count the amount of times I'd seen Hope awake in the past month on one goddamn hand.

I waited until I got back to the living room to pick up a pillow from the couch and smashed it with my fist across the room.

Not nearly as satisfying as punching Leander's face. Maybe not so sportsmanlike a thought considering the fucker was laid up with a broken foot. But it would have to do. I couldn't deal with being a good guy when I was so fucking exhausted.

I was doing the job on set, and I was doing it well. As the lead, I was in almost every frame.

The work was exhilarating. Exhausting, but exhilarating. And there was still time. The kids hadn't even been born yet. There'd be plenty of time to fix things. That was what I told myself as my face slammed into my pillow and I blinked asleep by the next breath.

<hr />

THE NEXT DAY on set during my half-hour break for lunch, I was scarfing down a panini while flipping the pages of the rewrite for the next scene, rapidly memorizing as I chewed. It was Venice so it wasn't like they could cart in trailers for us, no matter the star power. Instead, they'd set us up on a private rooftop lounge.

I sat on a comfortable outdoor couch with a gorgeous view of the ocean, but I was too focused on the pages in front of me to appreciate it at the moment. We were filming out of order and scenes were always being rewritten down to the last minute. Not that it was anything new. Thank fuck I had a good natural short-term memory. I could always spit back info if I crammed for quizzes the morning of.

"Mavros," one of the production-assistants called.

I glanced over my shoulder at a small Italian man scurrying my way, still half-attuned to my script. Others on the roof at the Italian version of a craft table looked our way. The assistant lowered his voice. "*Scusi*, Signor Mavros. A woman is here to see you. She says she is your girlfriend?"

I felt my eyebrows lift. *Hope was here?*

I dropped the pages to the couch and sprang up, feeling the first real wave of happiness in weeks.

I was about to call out her name but it died on my lips. Because instead of seeing Hope's plump, belly-rounded frame and wavy hair, it was—

Lena? Leander's clingy co-star from his last movie.

"Helena." My hands fisted at my sides and I had to consciously unclench them. "To what do I owe the pleasure?" *And who the fuck let you past security?* Some starstruck fuck who believed the tabloid fodder Lena loved to feed them, obviously.

I all but kicked myself. I should have realized as soon as the production assistant said *girlfriend* that he didn't mean Hope. Like always, I wasn't myself. I was pretending to be

Leander. God, I was doubly wishing I could punch the bastard, even if it wasn't his fault.

Lena's practiced smile immediately froze on her plastic face at my less than enthusiastic greeting.

I didn't think Leander would have been any more excited to see her, but he'd always had a little bit more of, what was it called... oh right, tact. At least where she was concerned, for some indecipherable reason.

I was happy to call a spade a fucking spade.

Helena was a witch. Not in the fun pagan way, either. More in the way where *witch* was the word gentleman substituted for women who were cruel to those they considered *less* than them.

Her eyes narrowed. She was fake inside and out, and she could spot others like her a mile away. So she'd been able to sense I wasn't genuine the first time I hurried into a press briefing late in Leander's stead.

I knew a lot of folks like her. They flocked to LA. Nothing narcissists loved more than being on screen, after all.

But she didn't call me out as she walked forward. We had an audience, and there was nothing Lena loved more than an audience. Even if this wasn't going the way she expected.

"What the fuck are you doing here?" she spit from between her still grinning teeth. She leaned in for a hug but I crossed my arms and pulled back.

I wasn't playing into this bullshit farce. The sooner I could pop her social media dream of her and Leander being a couple, the better. So I hoped every gossipy camera grip at the food tables across the rooftop was watching.

"Play along," she spat in my ear. "*Janus*. Unless you want me to announce to the whole rooftop who you are."

Annoyed as fuck, I put my arms around her in the barest imitation of a hug before dropping them again. She wrapped her arms around my waist and squeezed, giggling loudly in the performance of her life. I rolled my eyes before she pulled back, that beauty queen upbringing of hers still showing in the cornea-blinding Crest smile of hers. Dear fuck. She was such an over-actress. It was hard not to cringe. I worked with actual *professionals* every day.

She leaned in towards me, undoing her hair and shaking it out like she was in a shampoo commercial. I was sure that somehow, somewhere, there was a camera on us catching the moment. Which she was counting on, no doubt, since we were on an open rooftop.

Still grinning and talking through her teeth like she was a ventriloquist, she asked, "So where's Leander? Was that story about one of you breaking your leg even tr—"

But then she stopped, and I saw her working out the math in her head. "Holy shit, that's why you're here instead of him!"

I breathed out and tried to keep hold of my temper. So far, we'd managed to keep this secret in spite of everything—but that was only because the circle who knew it was extremely small and *extremely* well-paid: the two movie producers, our agent, Leander's doctor, the hospital administrator, plus obviously, Milo and Hope.

In Hollywood, information was everything. And Lena knowing this... fuck. It wasn't great.

"So what do you want, Lena?" I preferred to spend as little time in her presence as possible.

"Is Leander okay?" she demanded, for once not speaking through her teeth and looking genuinely concerned.

I breathed out again. I guessed beneath all those dragon scales there had to have been a beating heart at some point.

"Yeah, he's okay," I said quieter. "He did break his leg and it was bad. He's out of commission for another few months."

She blinked rapidly, obviously taking it in. Then she stopped and tilted her head at me incredulously. "And they thought *you* could do the job in his place?" Then she started laughing. Her high-pitched, cultivated laugh.

Yep, there it was. Lena would always be Lena.

"Okay, time to go," I said, putting my arm to the small of her back so it looked like I was being friendly as I urged her forwards, making it clear it was time to leave.

"Wait, wait, wait," she said rapidly as she turned and grabbed onto my arm, nails digging into my skin. "You need me even more now. I can help sell this. I'm serious. *Janus,*" she said louder than before, eyes hard.

I stopped in place, breathing out and not bothering to hide my frustration. "What the fuck, Helena?"

"I hate that name," she spat. "It's *Lena.*"

"Fine," I smiled hard. "Lena. What the fuck? Just let him go already. He doesn't want you."

"Says you."

"Says *him.* Jesus. Don't be this person. Pining after someone you never even had in the first place."

"How do you know what we had?" she hissed.

"Because I wasn't born fucking yesterday," I scoffed.

Her cheeks went red with fury. "So it's true? You only

like to fuck women together? How else would you even know who your brother fucks?"

I laughed and leaned in. "All you're admitting is that you never fucked him. And all I'm saying is that I know my brother has better taste."

Her hand whipped out and smacked me across the face. And then she froze, as if just realizing what she'd done.

"Kiss me," she whispered desperately, obviously panicking as she realized all the eyes on us.

I grimaced. "Fuck no."

"Kiss me or I tell them all you're Janus."

"What's your fucking damage?" I backed away. "How do you think you come back from that? I'm sorry that no one's ever told you *no* before and your career isn't what you want at the moment. But it's time to *let*"—I held my hands up— "*It*"—I bowed and finished, looking up at her—"*Go.*"

Around me, people started clapping and whooping as Lena backed up in humiliation. Several cameras were clearly up and filming us.

"He's not who you think he is!" Lena screamed, pointing at me.

At which point, I said loudly, "Security! This woman should never have been allowed on lot. I specifically did *not* put her on my approved list of visitors."

Lena screamed in indignation.

I leaned in. "If you don't want to be arrested for assault, which I'm pretty sure was caught on multiple cameras, I'd stop now."

Lena pointed a furious finger in my face and I winced back as if I was ducking from another blow. The growing crowd on the rooftop reacted around me: *Ooh!*

Lena looked around her, as if her public relations brain had just flicked back on, and I'd swear the fires of hell lit behind her eyes as she glared me down. Finger still pointed in my face, her hand trembled. "This isn't over," she whispered.

And then she spun and marched towards the exit.

Everyone started clapping.

The production assistant who had announced her arrival hesitantly came towards me, clutching an iPad to his chest.

"Signor Mavros? I'm so sorry to bother you, especially considering..." His head gestured towards Lena's retreating back and then he made a face. "I am sorry I did not double-check the approved visitor's list. So we were very, very vigilant when another woman showed up claiming to be a close family friend."

I looked down at my watch wondering what on earth I was about to face now.

But the assistant hurried to assure, "She's on the list, and we double-checked her name and ID."

I waved a hand to get to the point. "Who is it?"

But just then I looked up to the door that led to the elevator. The door pushed open as Hope stepped out onto the roof right as Lena reached for the doorknob.

TWENTY-THREE

HOPE

WHAT THE HELL was *she* doing here? The last I heard of Lena being in Italy was a month ago. Had she been here secretly visiting Janus on set the whole time? I thought they hated each other.

Her eyes lit up when she saw me and she waved her fingertips.

God, what a bitch.

Her eyes scoped me up and down. "Been hitting the pasta a little too hard, huh?" she laughed under her breath as we passed.

It would be unprofessional if my foot just *happened to* stick out and accidentally trip her, right?

When they go low... I grumbled to myself. And gritted my teeth, keeping my head up as I passed by. I clenched still tighter as her haughty laughter rang up the stairs behind her.

And you better believe I was pissed as I stalked across the roof towards Janus. I'd come here feeling so bad I hadn't seen him in what felt like weeks other than a glimpse here and there. So I thought I'd come and surprise him during lunch.

Only to find *her*.

My fists were clenched so hard, my fingernails bit into the flesh of my palms. And yet I knew I also had to keep myself in check because while Janus was my fiancé... *Leander* wasn't and we had to keep up pretenses.

Which was really frustrating at the moment because I wanted to scream at him *and* throw myself into his arms at the same time.

And, likely because of the pregnancy hormones, I also wanted to sit down right where I was standing and start bawling. Apparently, when you were pregnant, that was the solution to everything. Puppy on a commercial? Burst into tears. Leander says something even half-way sentimental or sweet? Burst into tears. Milo brings me back food from the market—tears.

But, uh... that wasn't the only pregnancy symptom that had been the most, er... noticeable lately.

See, there was this other... um... symptom? If you could call it that. 'Cause even though I was already knocked up, apparently my body's signals were all outta whack...

And I was hornier than I'd ever been in my life.

Really uncomfortably, unspeakably, unstoppably horny.

And yes, while I'd wanted to surprise Janus with lunch, well, I'd also hoped to...

But then when I'd shown up, the she-bitch was here and now my emotions felt all over the place. I was *still* horny even though Milo and Leander had fucked me this morning but I *also* felt like sitting down and crying.

Maybe Janus saw something of my dilemma on my face because he strode forward to meet me and put a hand to the small of my back. Which was ridiculously comforting even though I was still mad about Lena.

"I can explain about her," he whispered in my ear. Maybe he really could read me, or I was just shit at hiding my feelings lately. "Come on. Let's go somewhere without so many eyes. And God, it's good to see your face in daylight. I've missed you so much."

My heartbeat immediately amped down from fight or flight to a more regular rhythm. He always knew what to say to put me at ease.

But instead of relaxing, my suddenly whirling mind wondered if that was just part of the act. Janus was *too* perfect sometimes. So... what if it was just him playing a part? He was literally an *actor*. And I saw how well he slipped into being Leander so often and so well that no one but me could tell them apart.

Well, me *and* Lena.

I frowned.

As soon as we got to the stairwell down from the roof where no one else could hear, I turned to Janus. "Why was she here?"

Janus shook his head, looking frustrated. "She was just trying to stir up shit, like always."

"Does she come by set often?"

"What?" He looked surprised. "No."

I stared at him, wondering what to believe. Then I started down the stairs. I felt like crying again, and I was hungry. Hunger was the only other state of being I seemed to exist in besides horny and sleepy. I was a ball of basic instincts at the moment.

"Look, don't fuck with me," I snapped at Janus. Basic instincts also included irritation and anger. I didn't have the energy to hold them back or gussy them up with polite feminine demureness. "Is there something going on between you two?"

"No!" he exploded. "Jesus, what do you think of me?"

"I don't know. I never see you anymore!" I threw the hand not holding the railing into the air. "And I thought she left Italy last month."

"She came back." Janus said, hurrying to catch up so he was beside me on the narrow stairs. "I don't know. She's not getting the boost she hoped for off the last movie like Leander did? I think she's hoping hitching onto Leander like a leech will help her get more scripts."

The stairway opened into a hallway that Janus led me down. I followed because, well, where else was I gonna go? And he was saying the words I wanted to hear. But maybe he was just good at that. Some men were.

He suddenly turned the doorknob of a door in the hallway and pushed it open. Confidently, like he knew exactly where he was going. Except he also seemed surprised when it opened. He still strode right in.

"Janus, what are you—? Are we even allowed to be in here?"

I followed after him and looked around. The building was old, like everything here in Venice, with a huge, vaulted ceiling. It looked like some sort of library or study, with old leather-bound books lining the floor-to-ceiling bookshelves.

It was quiet and smelled exactly like you'd expect—like musty old books and rugs. All the furniture was antique, and the floor a dark burnished wood.

Janus just grinned at me. "Why not?"

Then he pulled me into the circle of his arms. "God, I've fucking missed you."

He let his forehead fall to mine, nuzzling for just a moment like he was savoring my scent before finally dropping his lips onto my lips.

Damn this man. I forgot what I was mad about. I forgot everything except the feel of his lips on mine and the firm feel of his arms around me as he backed me against the wall.

I groaned low into his mouth. *Yes*. This was exactly what I'd come here for. Before I'd seen the she-bitch. Remembering why I'd been mad soured my thoughts again, but only for a second.

Janus's explanation made sense. Of course Lena had come lurking on the hunt for Leander. She and Janus hated each other. I was being irrationally jealous because my hormones were all out of whack. And it would be stupid to waste this chance of *finally* having Janus to myself.

So I tossed my arms up around his neck and threw myself into him and the moment. His body was hard against mine.

And I did mean *hard*.

Yes, down there, but also his abs. And his *biceps*.

Both he and Leander had trained hard as they prepped for the movie, but Janus had apparently taken it to a whole different level since filming had begun. Meanwhile, I'd gotten used to Leander's body the last few weeks while he hadn't been able to train at all. So I'd gotten used to... softer.

Suffice to say, I noticed the difference when Janus put those rock-hard biceps of his to use, lifting me with his hands underneath my ass.

I shrieked a little before throwing my hand over my mouth. Janus nibbled at my fingers until I moved my hand back around his neck. And then he was devouring me with his mouth again. While *his* hand was moving my underwear beneath my skirt to the side—

"God, *yes*," I hissed in his ear as I felt the tip of his cock against my wet sex. I'd worn the skirt for easy access. I'd been imagining a scene like this during the entire taxi ride here and even still I couldn't have imagined it as hot as this. This gorgeous god of a man slamming me up against the wall and—

"Fuck, I've missed you," he broke from my lips long enough to repeat. He locked eyes with me, making love to me with his eyes even as he fed his huge, hard dick into me.

And then, still without dropping his eyes, he held me against the wall with one strong arm and slapped my ass with the other.

The sound of his palm hitting my flesh was loud and echoey in the palatial, perfectly preserved room. What we were doing seemed even naughtier because of the age and history you could feel in the walls of the building.

"You like the feel of me spanking your ass, don't you?" Janus growled through his teeth, and then he spanked me again. "You've missed your big ass jiggling when Daddy spanks you, haven't you?"

My pussy spasmed around the cock he'd just finished spearing me with. I was pinned to the wall by his big dick and his one arm while he spanked me again with his other hand. And then another time.

I clenched and writhed on him, my arms wrapped around his neck. "Please, Janus," I begged. "Please fuck me now." I was going to go crazy if he just stood there, not moving. Especially when he spanked me.

Every time he did, I *could* feel my big ass jiggle. And it jiggled not only my ass cheeks but *all* my fleshy bits down there. Including my swollen pussy. With each contact, he made the whole bottom half of my body vibrate around him, in fact.

It was so good I was about to cry.

The best fucking tears of my life as I begged Daddy to fuck me harder.

"Please," I asked as the first tear fell. "Fuck me."

Janus grinned so big at that. And then he dragged me down from the wall and spun me so that my ass was on a nearby desk. A desk that was obviously antique and ought to be treated well—

My ass landed on it and I couldn't care much more than that, because then Janus was bearing down on me. He tossed my left leg over his shoulder and then sank balls deep again.

His eyes rolled back in his head and then he closed them like he was savoring the feel of my pussy. Which made me spasm around him as I felt my orgasm approaching. It was like a wave, I could feel the first lapping ripples of it, and there it was in the distance. Oh, it was coming—

Janus ramped me higher and higher with every thrust. When he pushed in, he'd grind his groin against my clit, and I clawed against his back. Right when my climax was about to hit from every gorgeous bit of contact he was giving me—and ever since I'd hit the second trimester, I was a damn hair-trigger when it came to orgasming—he'd pull back.

I mean, it had only been a few minutes and I was ready to start coming. The pregnancy had made my body so sensitive, I could come for like twenty minutes straight these days. And I was all about giving myself over to what nature had in store for me, ya know? You gotta take the perks where you could find them.

But Janus had other plans, it seemed. He wanted to keep me on edge. Because just when I was about to tip over each time, he'd pull back. And then grin like the devil himself at me. He knew exactly what he was doing.

After so long away from each other, was he reminding me who was in charge here? Making me crave him so bad I'd come back more often?

Or trying to drive me so crazy that for once, I got the hell out of my head and just let my body do the driving?

That was my last thought as I did just that. I abandoned myself to him. I was simply the sensation he brought me. And he was masterful at playing my pleasure. It was wild to give myself completely over to him. To trust *anyone* that absolutely. But then, this was always the freedom Janus had given me from the very beginning.

He fucked me like we were dancing and when I finally gave in and let him truly and completely lead, it was... *magic*.

He grasped my hips hard and fucked me, strumming the bulbous head of his dick against my fat, swollen clit each time he entered me. I started to shudder on the desk as my orgasm overcame me uncontrollably.

The most intense pleasure-bordering-on pain absolutely wracked my spine. Down into my tailbone and then back up and out my skull.

Janus only increased his pace while I hissed and screeched out my pleasure, a noise so high-pitched that only dogs could hear.

When Janus thrust a couple last times and then bottomed out and came, he wrapped his arms so tight around me I could barely breathe. But I needed it too. He was making us one. As he was inside me, flooding me with his seed, his or his brother's babies growing in my belly, he wrapped me in him.

His hips spasmed a couple more times, getting the last of his cum out. But still he held me, tight as a mother holds her newborn child. Like any moment I might disappear if he let me go.

"I really love you," he whispered into my ear. "You know that, right? You know I've waited my whole life for you."

I swallowed down my sob. *Not now, emotions.* I didn't want to be a sobbing mess on him after we'd just had some of the most intense sex of my life. I hugged him even tighter as a couple tears squeezed out anyway.

"I love you too." It was all I could get out through my choked throat without breaking into tears but I hope he knew how much I meant it. I wanted to tell him how he was my game-changer. And how much I missed him lately. How things weren't the same without him. I wanted to tell him a thousand more things but his phone rang in his jeans he had shoved down over his ass.

"Fuck," he swore. "I gotta get that. It's probably them wanting me back on set."

I nodded quickly, burying my face in his chest so I could sneakily wipe my tears on his shirt. I swallowed hard. "Of course. I just stopped by to say hi."

He chuckled at that as he held me steady on the desk while he pulled out. His cum gushed out of me and all over the antique desk.

"Oh no!" I said, hopping off the desk and grabbing for my purse to find something to clean it with. But Janus just laughed and pulled me into a bear hug.

"Fuck, I love you."

I felt the flutters of the Beans doing flips in my belly then, as if wondering what all the fuss with my body shaking like that was about. And even though I heard voices just outside in the hall and I knew Janus's cum was still dripping off the expensive antique desk behind me, I could only laugh my ass off, too.

TWENTY-FOUR

HOPE

SO I WAS GRINNING as I headed down the rest of the stairs, still laughing about having barely cleaned up the desk in time and getting my clothes settled before the door pushed in and several men started speaking Italian at us.

I chuckled as I pushed the door open onto the back alley that led to the water taxis.

"Hey. You."

I looked up as a breeze full of salty sea-canal air hit my face.

And saw *her*. Again.

"What do you want?" I asked Lena, glaring as she walked towards me in the cleavage-baring blouse and capris she'd come to visit Janus in. Along with sky-high heels. How was she even standing up straight on these nubby cobblestones and not tripping on her ass?

I crossed my arms over my chest. Had she been here,

just waiting for me to come out? Or had she been waiting for Janus?

She smiled at me, like a snake baring its fangs. "I was hoping we could talk."

I shook my head. "Well, *you're* delusional. You don't deserve a second of my time." I turned to go.

She laughed, and it wasn't her cultured, beautiful one. "You actually think you know them? Either of them?"

I rolled my eyes and started walking towards the dock.

But she got in my way. I was happy to shoulder past her. I gave no shits. Pregnancy had given me a different perspective on things and I had absolutely zero tolerance anymore.

"Do you even know that it *wasn't* Janus who got into the accident all those years ago when they were teenagers? It was Leander."

What? Her words had me pausing in spite of myself.

"Then Leander convinced Janus to take the fall for him." Lena shrugged. "I mean, it was the obvious decision. Leander is by far the superior actor. And only one of them was realistically going to make it."

She propped her hand on her hip. And I was annoyed, because both of us had just realized that she'd captured me in place. I didn't want to stand here and listen to what she had to say, and I would bet my left kidney that neither Janus nor Leander would want me to either.

But still, my feet stayed frozen where I was.

Her thin little smile arched up on the edges. "So you *didn't* know. And Janus has been jealous of his brother's career ever since."

I definitely rolled my eyes at that and turned to leave again. It was ridiculous to listen to anything she had to say.

"Holy shit, it's not pasta that's made you fat. You're pregnant! Oh my God!" Her laughter echoed between the tall buildings lining either side of the canal. I looked around quickly, no doubt giving away the truth of what she'd said. But it was instinct at this point to check for eavesdroppers. No one was around.

"He finally did it." Lena shook her head, still smirking.

"What the hell are you even talking about?" I asked, pissed at both her and myself. I was two seconds away from leaving her in the dust.

It was only some terrible pit in my stomach that kept me anchored to the spot. Had the boys really lied to me about their pasts? I mean, even if Lena was telling the truth... after meeting their mom and learning all I had, who was I to judge a decision they'd made as teenagers?

Though it did sound bad that Leander would have let his own *brother* take the fall for him. Janus had spent six months in *juvie* for the crash. And his career... well, he didn't have one after he got out of jail. He was considered damaged goods. And Leander, the golden child. The talent.

A deep whisper inside me hissed: *you can never trust a man deep down. Just look at your own father*.

But even if Leander had done some disappointing things in the past, there was still Janus. He was a man I could trust. Janus had been nothing but honorable to me.

Then like she was reading my mind, Lena said, "I'm talking about lover boy Janus up there." A positively gleeful glint lit her eyes.

Just leave. She's baiting you and it's your fault if you stay and listen.

"Janus is the best man I've ever met in my life," I defended him.

She tilted her head and made a face like she pitied me. "Aw, look how sweet and stupid you are. I guess that's why it was so easy to dupe you."

I stood there silent, fuming. Not giving her the satisfaction of asking what she was talking about. She was obviously so delighted with herself she couldn't keep it back much longer. So I stood ramrod straight and glared at her.

And I was right, 'cause a moment later she said, "Don't you get it? God, you're gonna make me spell it out for you, aren't you?" She sighed dramatically. "Janus has been looking for a mommy for his fucked up little family to cement Leander to him. So he can never be left behind."

I started to roll my eyes again—

"You're like the fourth chick he's tried it with?" she kept on. "And I talked to the second woman, Sage, and she said she found Janus switching out her birth control for sugar pills."

"What?" I barked out with a laugh.

"Janus has wanted what he never had—a real family with a kid to bind them all together. It's fucking pathological with him. Doesn't it seem convenient how fast you got knocked up?"

TWENTY-FIVE

LEANDER

I WAS UP ON CRUTCHES, actually managing to leave my bedroom for the second time this week. Milo was right behind me in case I tipped or got in trouble, but still.

"Doing great, man."

"Yeah, yeah," I muttered, biting the side of my cheek as sweat broke out on my brow. I was determined to make it to the living room, though. The doctor had given me a certain timetable but I was determined to prove him wrong and improve faster than any other patient he'd ever had.

He'd never met a stubborn bastard like me before. Lying around in bed was not my fucking style. I was not a man to be waited on hand and foot, for one. I'd always earned my way in the world. Even when I'd been a teenage fuckwit, I'd still been a *workaholic* teenage fuckwit.

I'd been given a ton of privileges in life, and as screwed up as it was that our real-life parents died after America already loved our four-year-old on-screen persona... Well, it made our fame skyrocket. I didn't always know how to handle that.

Plenty of my peers around me had traded on less. Was I just an asshole profiting off my parents' tragedy? Even the idea pissed me off and made me work twice as hard with a fury to prove them all wrong. Even if it would take me years to ask who "them" even was and what exactly I was trying to "prove" anyway.

It still drove me to take every acting class I could, study harder than anyone around me, and take it more seriously. I gritted my teeth at how ridiculous I'd been, so self-serious and refusing to see I was just a kid in the shitty situation of having to grieve with the whole world watching. And then it felt like they all judged my grief. So-called reporters certainly asked about it in every interview when we were teenagers.

I always felt it—those eyes on me. And my incessant mind dug at me with the thoughts that tormented me worst: had I grieved *enough*? Had I even loved my parents at all? I barely remembered them. Maybe that meant I was broken in some fundamental way. If I wore black clothes and eyeliner, would it prove how sad I was?

I had just a single vague memory of my parents. And I'm not sure if it's just a memory *of* the memory at this point, I've recalled it so many times trying to cling to it. I see my mom's happy face laughing down at me from an open square in the ceiling as my dad lifted me up by my armpits into grampa's attic. Me and Janus were going to help Mom look for her childhood treasures in old boxes up there. There's this happy warmth that comes with the memory.

But again, I don't know if it's just something I've fabricated because of how much I *want* that feeling.

And then they died and suddenly a world that made sense toppled like a deck of cards.

Everything changed.

Except Jan and me. And the show, *Who's Counting Now?*

The set was familiar. At least we still went the same place every day. But then mean Mrs. Pappas who always ordered us around on set was suddenly trying to take us home with her. Milo had always been nice enough to us but we hated his mom. And then the rest of the grown-ups just let her take us. It didn't matter that Jan and me cried and kicked her and tried to run away.

That's when things got blurry for a few years. I just knew it wasn't good. And I remembered the closet Mrs. Pappas would lock us in for "acting up."

As if she knew that the worst punishment for Jan and me was to be separated. To be forced to be all alone in that dark, dark room. Milo too, because eventually he joined our little gang of two, even if he was too old for our games at first. I didn't realize how hard it had been for him till later, being excluded those first years. But Janus and I had grown up with a sort of twin-speak, especially when we were younger kids, where we had an uncanny knack for knowing what the other was thinking or feeling.

Later it bothered me. Like I wasn't even able to have my own thoughts to myself... But when we were young... Closer than two peas in a pod.

You'd never think it, to see us now.

I winced as I levered my body weight forward on the

crutches and felt pain lance up my leg. I placed the crutches and hefted myself forward again. One step and then another and another, ignoring the pain. Until I was not only into the living room but all the way to the window. Finally seeing a different fucking scene than the view from my bedroom.

From here I could see down onto the plaza, not just the back of another building.

I breathed out a little harder than I would have preferred, even as I enjoyed the warm of the sun on my face through the window. Two months ago I'd been training with elite athletes and professionals at the top of their game to star in a blockbuster, and now I wheezed at walking ten feet—

"Look," Milo said from beside me, pointing down at the plaza below. "She's back."

My heart leapt and not because of the stupid walk to the window. There she was. Hope's lithe figure striding across the bright plaza towards our building. Goddamn, this woman had done something to me. It was something else to find a person suddenly in your life who fulfilled every fantasy you never even knew you had. Something I never expected.

Obviously. I hadn't known how to handle her when I was suddenly presented with her in the flesh.

At some point in my past, something deep was hijacked in me. And then I just sort of detached... from everything around me. My brothers, my art, anything except going through the motions of existing. It felt like enough. It felt like success. Until Hope started chipping away at it. And then goddamn, when the news of her being pregnant hit—

I braced myself against the wall and ran my hand through my hair. I hoped I was fucking presentable.

So many tables had spun on their axes lately.

When we'd first met, Hope had been the one off-kilter, in pigtails and overalls when I'd been in my suit. I'd been trying to hide how damn attracted to her I was, anyway. And now look at us. Me simply glad to be on my feet when she came in and not laid out on my damn ass.

The door pushed open and Hope's brow was low. She looked up suddenly, like she was startled to find us in the living room. Which was fair, considering most the time I was holed up in the bedroom.

Her face quickly transformed from surprise to anger, though. Okay, that caught me off guard. I thought she'd be happy to see me up and around.

"What the fuck have you all been up to?" she asked, eyes furious as they skewered first me, then Milo.

"You'll have to be more specific," Milo said, in a tone I thought was fairly diplomatic for how pissed she looked. "What exactly are we supposed to have done now?"

Hope's eyes came back to me. "Did Janus take the fall for you when you were teenagers? When you crashed?"

I felt my eyes widen in alarm, which obviously gave me away. But what the fuck? Who had told her about that? *Janus?* That fucking bastard. I'd kill him.

"It's not what you think," I said, holding a hand up.

Her mouth dropped open. "It's not? Did you or did you not crash a car into a lady's house?"

I clenched my teeth. "I did."

"And did you spend even a day in jail for it?"

Milo's head swung back and forth between us like we

were a tennis match. "No, but—" he started and Hope's face swung his way. She looked betrayed. "You knew too?"

"Hope, what the fuck's really going on here?" I asked. "Who even told you about that?"

"How could you do that to Janus?" she asked, eyes huge like she didn't know me.

"He offered," I cut her off.

"Even if that's the truth—you *accepted?*" She looked at me like I was a monster. Considering some of the things Janus'd had to face down while he was locked up, maybe I was.

We weren't identical when he came back. That was for sure. Another inmate had smashed Janus's hand in a door, breaking three of the fingers on his left hand. At least it had been his left, he told me when he got out, with relief. Because he'd needed his right for swinging, in all the other fights he got into. Turned out lots of guys wanted a shot at the pretty boy actor once he got locked up.

I looked at Hope stone-faced.

"And Janus." She threw her hands up in the air, face bewildered and... something else I couldn't read.

"What?" I barked. What about the saint himself could she *possibly* be mad about?

She glared back at me, finger in my face. "Did he swap out my birth control pills with sugar ones because he fucking *wanted*"—she gestured with both hands angrily down at her pregnant belly—"*this* to happen!"

I cough-laughed out my surprise. And then froze, wondering if in one of Janus's more hypo-manic phases he could have— he *had* been really intense about Hope ever since she got here. But no way he would have...

My eyes shot to Milo, whose eyes had bounced straight to mine.

"What?" Hope asked, immediately clocking our reactions. "You think it's possible? Because I took the Plan B on time. I swear I did. And I read all the instructions for the pill and took it religiously, exactly when it said to. I didn't screw it up. And I googled it on the way here. The pill is supposed to be 99% effective if you take it right. So what the fuck?"

Milo blinked. "Janus wouldn't—"

"Stop standing up for them!" Hope turned on Milo. And I do mean *turned*. She was more furious than I'd ever seen her. Angrier than I'd even known a person could be.

"God!" she spat at Milo. "What did they ever even do for you? Give you their leftovers and drag you around the world as their entourage? Get a fucking *life*, Milo. Because it's time for me to do the same. I'm done being their convenient hang-along hole to fuck." She glared at me. "This arrangement is over. I quit."

Then she turned around, grabbed her bag from the floor beside the door, and left the same way she'd come in, door slamming after her with an ear-splitting *BANG*.

TWENTY-SIX

JANUS

I WAS FILMING one of the gondola scenes, so I was on set in Venice today. The bell signaling the end of the scene went off and I lowered the oar, stretching my arms. We'd been at it all day, setting up and trying to catch every moment of afternoon light.

"Signor Mavros. Signor Mavros!"

I held my hand over my eyes to look back towards the dock. The same assistant producer from the other day was hurrying towards the edge.

"Signor Mavros, I apologize. Emergency." He was holding out a phone towards me.

My internal alarm bells went off. Was it the babies? Had something happened?

I shoved the oar in the water and rowed as fast as I was capable back to the cobbled walkway. I jumped the last bit and grabbed for the phone at the same time.

"Hello?" I said, panicked. "What's wrong?"

"It's Hope," Leander's voice came through the line. Fuck. My whole chest constricted at her name.

"Is it the—"

"She left," he said and I took a breath.

"Are the babies okay?"

"What? Yes. I mean, I think so. She looked fine when she left."

I breathed out angrily. "Then what the fuck?" My brain tried to catch up with everything that had happened in the last sixty seconds. "She left? She went out somewhere?"

"No, she *left* left. She left us. Milo tried to follow her but she caught the only damn taxi in the plaza."

"What the fuck?" I strode away from the director and cinematographer—who'd stopped talking where they stood looking over footage together and glanced my way.

As soon as I was far enough away, I whispered furiously into the phone. "What the fuck did you do?"

"It wasn't me," Leander said back, obviously at the end of his rope. "Or not only me. Did you switch her birth control pills for fakes? Sugar pills?"

"What?" Every word out of his mouth since I'd picked up the phone sounded nuttier than the last. "No."

"You sure, Prince fucking Charming? Because apparently the pill is 99% effective or some shit. And now she thinks you switched them."

"The fuck? Why would she even—?" I shook my head. "I said I didn't do it." Although I couldn't say I hadn't been fucking deliriously happy when I heard the news. It was wish fulfillment. But that didn't mean I'd done something so she'd get that way. "Who even brought up switching out pills?" I asked.

"What I wanna know is what happened at lunch that she came back so pissed off? Talking this shit about pills and how she knew it was *you* who went to juvie instead of me?"

"What the—! *I* didn't tell her."

"Then what happened?"

"Nothing happened!" Then I stopped. "Okay, well, things *happened*. We had a great lunch and then after I took her down to a room and we—"

Leander cleared his throat and I rolled my eyes. I looked around set, as if Hope would magically appear like she had earlier back on the rooftop. But the sun was setting and if Hope had left Padua already—

What on earth could have happened between her leaving me flush-cheeked and satisfied and getting back home?

And then it hit like the bell they rang at the end of scenes. I froze where I stood. "Fucking Helena."

"Lena?" Leander's voice came sharp over the phone. "Lena was there?"

He said it as if it made everything make sense. Which made my hackles rise through the roof. "What did you tell that hell-bitch about our past?" I accused him.

A beat of silence, then he muttered, "Fuck. I got drunk one night after filming and admitted it wasn't me who went to juvie."

"You son of a bitch." I dragged the phone down from my face and it was hard not to pitch it into the canal.

How was the mother of our children supposed to trust us when we'd lied to her? I'd meant to get around to telling her the truth... someday. Probably. But with the babies coming, well, there didn't seem to be any real reason to dig up the past.

Some skeletons were best left dead and buried six feet deep.

"Have you tried her cell?" I asked. "Maybe if I call her and explain—"

"Can't. She dropped her phone right outside the front door. On purpose, I think. We've got to get to her and explain before she leaves Italy. The closest airport is the—"

"Marco Polo," I finished his sentence for him even though we both hated when we did that anymore. But right now I was happy if it meant I could get into action faster. Tourists who wanted to see Venice had moved enough traffic that it had warranted an international airport being built right on the mainland. So I was closer to where Hope was likely headed than Leander and Milo were. Depending on how far Hope's taxi had gotten her, anyway.

"How long ago did she leave?" I asked. "Maybe I can head her off."

"Now he's getting it. She left eight minutes ago."

"And you're just telling me now!" I hustled past movie crew. I'd make my excuses later, after I was already in a water taxi. "I'll get back to shore as quick as I can."

"Good. Because, Jan"—there was a rare note of vulnerability in my brother's voice—"we can't lose her."

I jogged towards where the water taxis were parked and flagged one down. "We won't."

I looked down at my phone. Padua was half an hour away from Venice. If I booked it, I could make it to the airport in twenty minutes. Right in time to catch Hope before she even went inside to buy a ticket

I'd explain that Lena had twisted everything up with her lies. And the part Lena *hadn't* lied about... well, I could explain that too. Eventually. A lot of it wasn't my story to tell, but if Hope just had patience with us...

I jumped on the boat and then the taxi driver and I sped off through the canals.

Hope was the mother of our children and the woman I loved.

I'd be the one on my knees this time, if that was what it took.

TWENTY-SEVEN

HOPE

QUIET TEARS SLIPPED DOWN my face as I paid the taxi driver in euros. The guy barely looked at me as he accepted the money. I was glad. I wasn't sure I could deal with an overly friendly driver at the moment.

He drove off the second I was out of the car clutching my bag. The only possessions I had in the world were on me. It made me feel very alone suddenly.

What was I doing? Was I seriously leaving behind everything I knew? My job? My... guys?

They aren't who you think they are. Lena's stupid high-pitched voice echoed in my head.

She's a liar. You know she likes to stir up trouble.

I sighed as I stood there on the sidewalk. The sun had set on the ride here. As I paused indecisively, people hurried past me on all sides as the sky cracked with thunder and it began to rain.

Because of course it did.

Well, at least it matched my mood.

I wrapped my hands low around my pregnant belly.

"Little beans, it looks like it's just you and me," I whispered, my voice wavering as I shivered from the sudden cool of the summer storm. I couldn't stand out here trying to decide what to do, so I hurried inside.

The thing was, I hated this feeling. This not knowing what was going on and being punched with information like the last idiot standing. I thought I'd finally broken through and they'd let me in. One of them was the father of these twins in my belly, for God's sake!

But they kept secrets from me. I still wasn't fully on the inside.

Even if everything Lena said had been lies—and Leander already admitted it wasn't—but even if it could be chalked up as some big misunderstanding...

If I stepped back and looked at the situation I'd gotten myself into... I let my head fall forward, rain spattering my hair and the back of my neck.

That was just it.

I'd been running headfirst into a storm this entire time. From the word go. From the very moment Milo called me that day and invited me over for the insanity that was that first unorthodox interview.

Everything had happened so quickly, one thing after another. And then I was pregnant and Leander stopped me from leaving and—

By the end, I'd convinced myself we were making it work.

But really, wasn't I just doing what I'd done my whole

life growing up? *I* was the one straining to make everyone a happy, happy family regardless of how it was affecting me. I hadn't even stopped to think about how I felt about everything. I *wanted* it to work. Their bodies were a comforting solidity at night. They said the right things, on occasion anyway. So if at times I was the putty holding it all together, navigating tempers and walking the tightrope between egos...

All because what? The thought of being on my own alone with this baby, no, these *babies*—God, I could still barely wrap my head around the fact that there were *two*—

Getting this job and then going off with Milo and the twins for the summer to Italy was supposed to be me taking a risk for once and living a fantasy.

Well, it had definitely been risky. And this was suddenly all too real. Now I was about to enter my third trimester with freaking *twins*.

And while Leander had been sweet lately and so open about his past—I snorted. He really was a good actor. Because what I'd taken for vulnerability couldn't have really been all *that* honest if he'd been covering the fact that that his brother had taken the fall for him back then. It was true he'd never mentioned anything about juvie and I'd never asked, but still... We'd talked about the accident, and he'd lied straight to my face.

Then there was Leander's past behavior to consider.

Yes, he was being nice now. He was also laid up with his leg in a cast, relying on me as his attractive nursemaid who liked to find creative ways to fuck him in spite of his injury. But what about when our lives went back to restful and it wasn't constantly on me to serve him and his needs twenty-four-seven? When we had not one, but two needy little babies who required attention?

Would he go back to being a jerk, leaving me to pick up all the slack and be the grownup in the relationship?

And then there was Janus. It seemed so ridiculous to think of Janus doing anything like what Lena said he had. But still. My hand went to my belly. I'd checked and double-checked about taking the birth control. Though it seemed like I was always reading about how someone or other got pregnant on the pill. I could just be paranoid because of what Lena said.

But Janus... I frowned. He'd just been so sure since the beginning. So sure of what he wanted. That this odd little family unit could work even before there were actual *children* involved.

And I'd been so scared when I first got pregnant, I'd allowed Janus's sureness to be my sureness. It was the comforting dynamic of our play. He led and I followed.

Yes, of course, this was a sane thing to do, I let myself accept without question.

Yes, of course, it would all work out.

Yes, of course, fucking three men and then having their twins... while not knowing who the father is... It was a great life path. Also an aces career move. Especially as a publicist to movie stars. No way that could ever blow up in our faces. We'd *really* thought that one through like mature adults before bringing small lives into this world.

I was breathing in and out so rapidly now I was pretty sure I was near to either hyperventilating or having a panic attack. Which one was it when you breathed so fast that suddenly you felt like you couldn't breathe at *all* and then your heart went bang BANG *BANG* really, really loud in your ears???

That one.

I was having that one.

"Are you all right, Signora?" asked an older woman with kindly lines grooved in her face.

I gasped in a huge gulp of breath and the world zoned back in around me.

I nodded and hugged my purse to my chest. "Tickets?" I asked hoarsely, trying to focus on speaking instead of the panic. "Where can I buy tickets?"

Whatever was going on between the guys and me, I could figure out later. I just needed to get the hell out of here.

My body was sending me clear signals in the fight or flight department. These guys could have their fucked-up little dynamic. I needed to go decompress, figure some shit out, and finish growing some babies.

Somewhere calm.

The woman smiled kindly and pointed to a kiosk I hadn't seen because of people passing. But now that I saw it, it was obvious.

"*Grazie,*" I said, with a little wave.

I'd talk to the guys. Later. On the phone.

Where I wouldn't be immediately intoxicated with their presence. I couldn't think straight. I couldn't tell what was lies and what was truth anymore. I couldn't tell if I'd been manipulated into this situation, the way I used to see my dad do to Mom anytime she even thought about growing a backbone and spiting him.

Daddy was a genius manipulator. If Mama was upset

about one of the many things he'd done that wasn't fair, or taken without asking, he'd find something about the *tone* Mama used when she confronted him. Then he'd turn the fight into a discussion about how actually *she* was the one in the wrong, because she couldn't speak sweet to him. And what he'd done wrong would never be mentioned again. He just kept turning it on her.

And she couldn't see the pattern even though he did it over and over and *over* again.

I shook my head, striding towards one of the many desk kiosks to ask for information even as I reached for my wallet in my purse.

I always swore to myself I would never ever be my mama. Lies were red flags. They'd lied. And I knew I had no objectivity in my current situation because of the pregnancy. Hormones, not to mention the foolhardy hopes and dreams that had been blossoming the last couple months had blinded me and I'd been...

Foolish.

"Hi," I said to a nice-looking young woman with a streak of pink in her hair standing behind the desk of the large sign that said *acquistare il del treno* and underneath in English, *buy train tickets here.*

I swallowed my tears and then infused my voice with as much strength as possible. "One-way train ticket to Milan."

Read on for a preview of book 3: *Who's Your Alpha Daddy*, Complete Season 3, available at
https://geni.us/WhYoAlDa-EN-n**.**

*(please note: putting too short a preorder date gives *me* panic attacks cause I can't handle deadlines for mental health reasons. So for all our sakes, lol, I'm putting the official date out a bit and then will release it sooner (these are the mental games we wage with ourselves, or at least I do, lol). Because while authors cannot move pre-order dates *back* without a year-long penalty, we can move them *up* and get the book to you sooner :)

FIRST CHAPTER PREVIEW:

Chapter 1
   HOPE

"SO YOU JUST LEFT?" Mikayla, my once client and current best friend in all the world stared at me open mouthed as she stuck her hands out again towards my stomach. We were standing in the foyer of her expensive hotel suite in Milan. She paused a hand-span away and lifted her eyebrows, asking permission.

I sighed and laughed tiredly, grabbing her hands and putting them on my belly. "Yes. I just left. Well, first I ditched my phone. After everything I learned about them, I wouldn't put it past one of those bastards to have put a tracking app on it. It did make for a boring train ride over here, though. Can I finally come inside now?"

"Sure, but," she frowned, her palms still pressed against

my tummy. "I was hoping I'd feel something. When my cousin was pregnant, I could feel the baby moving. Like a little alien inside her."

I hugged her while she kept palming my stomach, searching for my alien. "Oh my God, I've missed you."

When I finally pulled away, I sighed and dropped my bag to the floor. "Tell me you have... shit, I was about to say vodka." I put the palms of my hands to my tired eyes. They felt like they'd been pummeled. "It is *criminal* not to allow pregnant women alcohol or caffeine!"

"I still can't believe you're gonna pop out twins." Mikayla hadn't stopped staring fixedly down at my stomach ever since she'd opened the door.

"Yeah, yeah." I reached down into my bag and pulled out some acetaminophen. I carried it everywhere with me these days for my aches and pains.

It was just my normal bag, but I always packed it like I was Mary Poppins. I could pull out anything on a moment's notice. It had started feeling like it was filled with bricks about eight blocks ago.

Fucking Italy with its culture of *walking* everywhere. They clearly had not had pregnant women in mind when designing this damn place. I mean, yes to the food, but Jesus, I needed one of those sexy little scooters I saw some people zipping around in if we stayed much longer.

And I guess that was the question, wasn't it? Was I staying? ... or going for good?

"Will you let me in the actual suite already?" I laughed tiredly, pushing past Mikayla.

She'd texted me last week that she'd be here in Milan for a fashion show. At the time I said I hoped I'd be able to get out to see her. Serendipitous timing. Especially since I hadn't even mentioned it yet to any of the guys. I kept meaning to but it slipped my mind.

And now she was my refuge.

"Aww, yeah. Come in, Mama. Tell me all about it. I've got gelato."

And just like that, I started bawling and telling her the whole tale as she led me to the couch and immediately came back with gelato, just as promised. Chocolate. My favorite.

"That horrid cow," she said when I got to the part about Lena.

I nodded, wiping at my messy face with the sleeve of my shirt. "I know, right? Can we put her picture up and throw darts at it?"

Mikayla nodded. "We'll find the ugliest ones on TMZ and print them out."

"Oh, goody." I clapped through my tears.

She gave me a one-sided shoulder hug. "It's been a lot, it sounds like."

I nodded, leaning my head on her shoulder and sinking there.

"You know what you need?"

I shook my head, eyes wet.

"All mamas and mamas-to-be deserve pampering! It sounds like these idiots have been running you ragged. Have you even been taking any me-time?"

I sniffled and tried to think. "Leander broke his leg, and he really needs a lot of help, and then there's all the publicity, and it's all just been so nonstop—"

"Zip it!" Mikayla made a motion across my lips with her fingers. "All I'm hearing are excuses for you not taking care of yourself. You're growing a *person* inside you! You could lay on a couch all day and be the most productive person I know! I know this is an insane concept to someone like you —but it's called taking a day *off*."

I tried to shake my head. "I'm in Italy. My whole life is a day off."

"Horseshit. Everything you've described to me sounds stressful as hell. Come on. You were there when I told you about all the therapy I went through. How even when good stuff is happening—or shit that *should* be good—on the outside, it doesn't mean you aren't allowed to have all sorts of different feelings about it on the inside."

I pulled back at her and stared. "Damn. When did you go and get all grown up? Where'd the little girl with a retainer go?"

"Dear *God*, if you ever let that out, I'll sue you for breach of your NDA," she said, face serious in the way only a drama queen could do.

I punched her in the side. "You're such a bitch."

She broke character and grinned at me, hugging me again and dragging me against her. "And you *love* me for it. Now let's go get matching massages and loosen you the fuck up!"

"Sleep first," I cried. "I was on the train for over three hours. And after today..." I shook my head. God, I'd never experienced a day full of so many ups and downs. I was bone-tired and couldn't imagine how I'd made it this long without passing out somewhere. I imagined the umbilical cord in my stomach like a power cord plugged into my energy system, sucking every ounce of extra momentum away.

Just then Mikayla's phone rang. She pulled it out of her leggings pocket and looked at the screen, then her eyes flew to mine. "It's *you*." She held it out to me and I saw my number and ID flash across the screen.

I gulped. "It has to be them. They found my phone and they must be calling all my contacts trying to find me."

"Do you want me to answer?"

My heartbeat fluttered and I shook my head no in a panic. *No.* I knew I'd have to deal with them eventually. But then I closed my eyes. Maybe that wasn't fair. I *was* carrying their babies. Was it really okay to just disappear because I was out of sorts and not sure what I wanted at the moment? I wasn't sure I was strong enough to deal with their rationalizations and explanations at the moment.

I needed what I wasn't sure I was strong enough to ask them for: time off. Time off from all of them. A vacation. Time to rest and get my head on straight.

"Text them back," I said to Mikayla impulsively. "Tell them I'm fine but I need a couple weeks to myself. And that I'll contact them soon."

Mikayla's eyes were big as she watched me, thumbs hovering above the phone. "You sure?"

I took a deep breath. "Sure."

Then I went and crashed on her sumptuous hotel bed.

Only to wake to loud, brutal knocking several hours later.

I roused and blinked my eyes open to one of the twins' loud voices through the door from the living room, demanding to see me.

Get Who's Your Alpha Daddy: Complete Season 3
now so you don't miss a thing!
https://geni.us/WhYoAlDa-EN-n
Please note: date likely to be moved up closer.

FOR A BONUS SCENE set during mid-book 2, go
to https://bookhip.com/VFCTDGD. *A night Janus actually makes it home early enough from filming while everyone is awake. One more peek inside Janus's head. And naturally, seggsy shenanigans* :)

WANT to check out Stasia's already completed Amazon Top 50 Bestselling WHY CHOOSE Marriage Raffle Series? https://geni.us/MaRaBx-EN-w

---

Nix never put his name in the marriage raffle for a reason.

He doesn't need a woman.

There aren't that many to go around these days.

He has his job as head of the Security Squadron and it's all he needs.

He looks out for the township.

He protects the few women there are left.

But when his name is called to be one of the five husbands to the woman rescued from the badlands, he doesn't speak up to correct the error.

Because Audrey's like no one he's ever met before.

Fiesty. That's the name for her.

Not like so many of the women they've brought back before.

She's not broken.

She might be just the woman to handle a rough, brutal man like him.

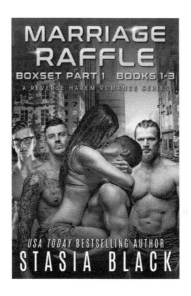

And JOIN MY NEWSLETTER for first peeks, new release news, ARCs, and more. No spamming, ever!

https://geni.us/SBA-nw-cont-w

ALSO BY STASIA BLACK

REVERSE HAREM ROMANCES

MARRIAGE RAFFLE SERIES

Theirs To Protect [https://geni.us/Th2Pr-EN-w]

Theirs To Pleasure [https://geni.us/Th2Pl-EN-w]

Theirs To Wed [https://geni.us/Th2We-EN-w]

Theirs To Defy [https://geni.us/Th2De-EN-w]

Theirs To Ransom [https://geni.us/Th2Ra-EN-w]

Marriage Raffle Boxset Part 1 [https://geni.us/MaRaBx-EN-w]

Marriage Raffle Boxset Part 2 [https://geni.us/MaRaBx-2-EN-w]

WHO'S YOUR DADDY SERIES

Who's Your Daddy Season 1 [https://geni.us/WhYoDa1-EN-w]

Who's Your Daddy Season 2 [https://geni.us/WhYoBaDa-EN-w]

Who's Your Daddy Season 3 [https://geni.us/WhYoAlDa-EN-w]

FREEBIE

Their Honeymoon [https://BookHip.com/QHCQDM]

DARK CONTEMPORARY ROMANCES

BREAKING BELLES SERIES

Elegant Sins [https://geni.us/ElSi-EN-w]

Beautiful Lies [https://geni.us/BeLi-EN-w]

Opulent Obsession [https://geni.us/OpOb-EN-w]

Inherited Malice [https://geni.us/InMa-EN-w]

Delicate Revenge [https://geni.us/DeRe-EN-w]

Lavish Corruption

Dark Mafia Series

Innocence [https://geni.us/Innocence-EN-w]

Awakening [https://geni.us/Awakening-EN-w]

Queen of the Underworld [https://geni.us/QuOfThUn-EN-w]

Persephone & Hades (Box Set) [https://geni.us/InBx-EN-w]

Beauty and the Rose Series

Beauty's Beast [https://geni.us/BeBe-EN-w]

Beauty and the Thorns [https://geni.us/BeNThTh-EN-w]

Beauty and the Rose [https://geni.us/BeNThRo-EN-w]

Billionaire's Captive (Box Set) [https://geni.us/BiCa-EN-w]

Love So Dark Series

Cut So Deep [https://geni.us/CuSDe-EN-w]

Break So Soft [https://geni.us/BrSSo-EN-w]

Love So Dark (Box Set) [https://geni.us/LoSDa-EN-w]

Stud Ranch Series

The Virgin and the Beast [https://geni.us/ThViNThBe-EN-w]

Hunter [https://geni.us/Hunter-EN-w]

The Virgin Next Door [https://geni.us/ThViNeDo-EN-w]

Reece [https://geni.us/Reece-EN-w]

Jeremiah [https://geni.us/Jeremiah-EN-w]

Taboo Series

Daddy's Sweet Girl [https://geni.us/DaSwGi-EN-w]

Hurt So Good [https://geni.us/HuSGo-EN-w]

Taboo: a Dark Romance Boxset Collection [https://geni.us/Taboo_Bx-EN-w]

Vasiliev Bratva Series

Without Remorse [https://geni.us/WiRe-EN-w]

Freebie

Indecent: A Taboo Proposal [https://geni.us/SBA-nw-cont-w]

Sci-fi Romances

Draci Alien Series

My Alien's Obsession [https://geni.us/MyAlOb-EN-w]

My Alien's Baby [https://geni.us/MyAlBa-EN-w]

My Alien's Beast [https://geni.us/MyAlBe-EN-w]

ABOUT THE AUTHOR

STASIA BLACK grew up in Texas, recently spent a freezing five-year stint in Minnesota, and now is happily planted in sunny California, which she will never, ever leave.

She loves writing, reading, listening to podcasts, and has recently taken up biking after a twenty-year sabbatical (and has the bumps and bruises to prove it). She lives with her own personal cheerleader, aka, her handsome husband, and their teenage son. Wow. Typing that makes her feel old. And writing about herself in the third person makes her feel a little like a nutjob, but ahem! Where were we?

Stasia's drawn to romantic stories that don't take the easy way out. She wants to see beneath people's veneer and poke into their dark places, their twisted motives, and their deepest desires. Basically, she wants to create characters that make readers alternately laugh, cry ugly tears, want to toss their kindles across the room, and then declare they have a new FBB (forever book boyfriend).

Join Stasia's Facebook Group for Readers for access to deleted scenes, to chat with me and other fans and also get access to exclusive giveaways:

Stasia's Facebook Reader Group

Want to read an EXCLUSIVE, FREE novella, Indecent: a Taboo Proposal, that is available ONLY to my newsletter subscribers, along with news about upcoming releases, sales, exclusive giveaways, and more?

Get **Indecent: a Taboo Proposal**

When Mia's boyfriend takes her out to her favorite restaurant on their six-year anniversary, she's expecting one kind of proposal. What she didn't expect was her boyfriend's longtime rival, Vaughn McBride, to show up and make a completely different sort of offer: all her boyfriend's debts will be wiped clear. The price?

One night with her.

Connect with me on social media!

Website: stasiablack.com

tiktok.com/@stasiablackauthor

facebook.com/StasiaBlackAuthor

twitter.com/stasiawritesmut

instagram.com/stasiablackauthor

amazon.com/Stasia-Black/e/B01MY5PIUH

bookbub.com/authors/stasia-black

goodreads.com/stasiablack

Printed in Great Britain
by Amazon